CHRONICLES OF ANCIENT DARKNESS

GHOST HUNTER

FAR NORTH ↑

C, NARWAL,
N, WALRUS CLANS

RAVINE

MOUNTAIN OF
THE WORLD
SPIRIT

ICE
CLIFFS

REE SLOPES

ICE
RIVER

THE
DEEP
FOREST

AUROCH, LYNX,
FOREST HORSE,
RED DEER,
BAT CLANS

THE HIGH MOUNTAINS

CHRONICLES OF ANCIENT DARKNESS

GHOST HUNTER

MICHELLE PAVER

BOOK
SIX

KATHERINE TEGEN BOOKS
An Imprint of HarperCollins*Publishers*

Katherine Tegen Books is an imprint of HarperCollins Publishers.

Chronicles of Ancient Darkness: Ghost Hunter
Text copyright © 2009 by Michelle Paver
Illustrations copyright © 2009 by Geoff Taylor

Library of Congress Cataloging-in-Publication Data
Paver, Michelle.
    Ghost hunter / Michelle Paver. — 1st U.S. ed.
        p.   cm. — (Chronicles of ancient darkness ; bk. 6)
    Summary: To fulfill his destiny, Torak must defy demons and tokoroths,
navigate through the Gorge of the Hidden People, and battle the evil Eagle
Owl Mage.
    ISBN 978-0-06-072840-3 (trade bdg.)
    ISBN 978-0-06-072841-0 (lib. bdg.)
    [1. Prehistoric peoples—Fiction.   2. Demoniac possession—Fiction.
3. Human-animal communication—Fiction.   4. Fantasy.]   I. Title.
PZ7.P2853Gh   2010   2009020616
[Fic]—dc22   CIP
                                                                AC

Typography by Amy Ryan
10 11 12 13 14   LP/RRDB   10 9 8 7 6 5 4 3 2 1
❖
First U.S Edition
First published in Great Britain in 2009 by Orion Children's Books,
a division of the Orion Publishing Group Ltd.

CHRONICLES of ANCIENT DARKNESS

GHOST HUNTER

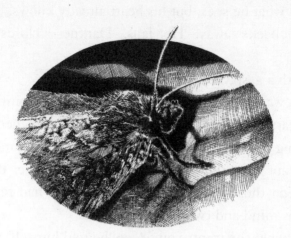

ONE

Torak doesn't want to enter the silent camp.

The fire is dead. Fin-Kedinn's axe lies in the ashes. Renn's bow has been trodden into the mud. The only trace of Wolf is a scatter of paw prints.

Axe, bow, and prints are dusted with what looks like dirty snow. As Torak draws closer, gray moths rise in a swarm. Grimacing, he flicks them away. But as he moves off, they settle again to feed.

At the shelter, he halts. The doorpost feels sticky. He catches that sweet, cloying smell. He dare not go in.

It's dark in there, but he glimpses a heaving mass of gray moths—and beneath it, three still forms. His mind rejects what he sees, but his heart already knows.

He backs away. He falls. Darkness closes over him. . . .

With a gasp, Torak sat up.

He was in the shelter, huddled in his sleeping-sack. His heart hammered against his ribs. His jaws ached from grinding his teeth. He had not been asleep. His muscles were taut with the strain of constant vigilance. But he had seen those bodies. It was as if Eostra had reached into his mind and twisted his thoughts.

It's what she wants you to see, he told himself. It isn't true. Here is Fin-Kedinn, asleep in the shelter. And Wolf and Darkfur and the cubs are safe at the resting place. And Renn is safe with the Boar Clan. *It isn't true.*

Something crawled along his collarbone. He crushed it with his fist. The gray moth left a powdery smear and a taint of rottenness.

At the back of the shelter, another moth settled on Fin-Kedinn's parted lips.

Torak kicked off his sleeping-sack and crawled to his foster father. The moth rose, circled, and flitted out into the night.

Fin-Kedinn moaned in his sleep. Already, nightmares were seeping into his dreams. But Torak knew not to wake him. If he did, the evil images would haunt the Raven Leader for days.

Torak's own vision clung to him like the moths'

unclean dust. Pulling on leggings, jerkin, and boots, he left the shelter.

The Blackthorn Moon cast long blue shadows across the clearing. Around it, the breath of the Forest floated among the pines.

A few dogs raised their heads as Torak passed, but the camp was quiet. One had to know the Raven Clan as well as he did to perceive how wrong things were. The shelters clustered like frightened aurochs about the long-fire which burned through the night. Saeunn had ringed the clearing with smoking juniper brands mounted on stakes, in an attempt to ward off the moths.

In the fork of a birch tree, Rip and Rek roosted with their heads tucked under their wings. They slept peacefully. So far, the gray moths had only blighted people.

Ignoring the ravens' gurgling protests, Torak gathered them up and went to sit by the long-fire, his arms full of drowsy, feathered warmth.

In the Forest, a stag roared.

When he was little, Torak loved hearing the red deer bellow on misty autumn nights. Snuggled in his sleeping-sack, he would gaze into the embers and imagine he saw tiny, fiery stags clashing antlers in fiery valleys. He'd felt safe, knowing that Fa would keep the dark and the demons away.

He knew better now. Three autumns ago, on a night

such as this, he had crouched in the wreck of a shelter, and watched his father bleed his life away.

The stag fell silent. Trees creaked and groaned in their sleep. Torak wished someone would wake up.

He longed for Wolf; but howling for him would disturb the whole camp. And he couldn't face the long walk to find the pack. How has it come to this? he wondered. I'm afraid to go into the Forest alone.

"This is how it starts," Renn had told him half a moon before. "She sends something small, which comes in the night. Something you can't keep out. And the gray moths are only the beginning. The fear will grow. That's what she feeds on. That's what makes her strong."

Far away, an eagle owl called: *oo-hu, oo-hu.*

Torak grabbed a stick and jabbed savagely at the fire. He couldn't take much more of this. He was ready: he had a quiverful of arrows, and his fingertips ached from sewing his winter clothes. He'd ground the edges of his axe and knife so sharp they could split hairs.

If only he knew where to find her. But Eostra had hidden herself in her Mountain lair. Like a spider, she had cast her web across the Forest. Like a spider, she sensed the least tremor in its farthest strand. She knew he would hunt her. She wanted him to try. But not yet.

Scowling, Torak tried to lose himself in the glowing embers. He woke to a voice calling his name.

The logs had collapsed. The ravens were back in their

tree. He hadn't dreamed that voice. He had heard it. It was familiar—unbearably so. It was also impossible.

Rising to his feet, Torak drew his knife. When he reached the ring of juniper brands that protected the camp, he paused. Then he squared his shoulders and walked past them into the Forest.

The moon was bright. The pines floated in a white sea of mist.

Above him on the slope, something edged out of sight.

Torak's breath came fast and shallow. He dared not follow. But he had to. He climbed, scratching his hands as he pushed through the undergrowth.

Halfway up, he stopped to listen. Nothing but the stealthy drip, drip of mist.

Something tickled his knife-hand.

At the base of his thumb, a gray moth fed on a bead of blood.

"Torak . . ." A pleading whisper from the trees.

Dread reached into Torak's chest and squeezed his heart. This wasn't possible.

He climbed higher.

Through the swirling mist, he glimpsed a tall figure standing by a boulder.

"Help me . . ." it breathed.

He blundered toward it.

It melted into the shadows.

It had left no tracks; only a branch, faintly swaying. But behind the boulder, Torak found the remains of a fire. The logs were cold, covered in ash. He stared at them. They'd been laid in a star pattern. This couldn't be. Only he and one other person built their fires that way.

Look behind you, Torak.

He spun around.

Two paces away, an arrow had been thrust into the earth.

Torak recognized the fletching at once. He knew the one who had made this arrow. He wanted desperately to touch it.

He tried to lick his lips, but his mouth was dry.

"Is it you?" he called, his voice rough with fear and longing.

"Is it you? . . . *Fa?*"

TWO

"It may not have been him," said Fin-Kedinn.

"It was Fa," said Torak, rolling up his sleeping-sack. "His arrow, his fire, his voice. His spirit."

Fin-Kedinn prodded the earth in front of the shelter with his staff. "Voices can be mimicked. Those who knew him remember how he woke his fires. As for that arrow—"

"I know," Torak cut in, "anyone could have found it. Because I left him in the Forest. No rowan branches, no chants. Just a botched attempt at Death Marks. No wonder he's not at peace."

Grabbing strips of dried meat from the cross-beams,

he crammed them in his food pouch. *The dried deer meat,* his father had gasped as he lay dying. *Take it all.* But in his haste, Torak had left it behind.

"You were twelve summers old," Fin-Kedinn said quietly. "You did your best."

"It wasn't enough. Now he's begging me for help."

"Or Eostra wants you to think so."

Torak stiffened. These days, few dared say that name out loud.

"This is what she does," said the Raven Leader. "She steals into thoughts and dreams. She breeds fear."

"I know."

"Do you? Do you have any idea how powerful she is? She has tokoroths at her command. She has the fire-opal. All the other Soul-Eaters were afraid of her. And you want to seek her alone."

Torak paused. The mist had thickened to fog, and in the wakening camp, people loomed and vanished like ghosts. He saw pinched, terrified faces. He wondered if the fog had been sent by Eostra.

Opening his medicine pouch, he found the chunk of black root which he'd begged from Saeunn, in case he needed to spirit walk. But what use was that against the Eagle Owl Mage?

"Maybe you're right," he said. "Maybe what I saw last night was her doing. Fa was a Soul-Eater for a time.

Maybe she's got some hold over his spirit. But I have to do something."

"Not yet. It's been only days since the moths came. Not even Saeunn has seen anything like them. I've had word from Durrain of the Red Deer—she agrees with me. We must gather the clans. If we don't—if we give in to fear—we fall into Eostra's hands."

"I can't wait any longer!" Torak burst out. "Again and again I've wanted to set off, and you've always said no! The Mountains are vast, you said; you could search your whole life and never find her. But now we're under attack. Who knows what she'll send next? It's my destiny to face her, Fin-Kedinn. Must I wait till she has the whole Forest in her grip?"

"So what would you do, head off for the Mountains and trust to luck?"

"I won't need to! She wants my power. When she's ready, she'll tell me where she is."

"When she's ready, Torak! When she's got you alone. When it's too late. No. I won't let you go."

"You can't stop me."

They faced each other. Fin-Kedinn was broader and stronger, but Torak no longer had to look up to him.

Taking his medicine pouch, Torak yanked the drawstring tight. "When Renn gets back, tell her I'm sorry. It's too dangerous for her to come with me. At least that's one decision you'll approve of," he added with some bitterness. Since he'd turned fifteen—the age at which clan law permitted a boy to seek a mate—it had seemed as if Fin-Kedinn were trying to keep them apart.

Casting away his staff, Fin-Kedinn took a few paces, then returned. "I understand the urge to contact the dead. Believe me I do; when your mother died . . . But Torak, it must be *resisted*. The living and the dead can't be together. It casts a blight on the living; it drags them down into madness!"

He spoke with startling vehemence, and for a moment, Torak was shaken. Then he shouldered his quiver and bow and took up his axe. "He's my father," he said.

"*Your* father. *Your* destiny. But this is not only *your* battle! This threatens us all!"

"That's why I have to leave. I can't do nothing any longer."

Torak left the Raven camp soon afterward. The fog oppressed his spirits, but he saw no gray moths, and felt no immediate menace as he headed east.

Around midday, the fog lifted and the sun came out. Beads of moisture sparkled on amber bracken and silvergreen beard-moss. The last of the willowherb gleamed purple beneath golden birch and blazing rowan: the Forest's final burst of brilliance before going to sleep for the winter. It had been a good autumn for nuts and berries, and the undergrowth rustled with small creatures enjoying the feast. Jays squabbled over acorns. Squirrels buried hazelnuts in the leaf mold.

Rip and Rek flew past, making woodpecker noises and pretending to ignore Torak. They were in a sulk at having to leave the Raven camp, where they'd grown fat on offerings, especially Rip. He'd lost a wing-feather fighting the Oak Mage in the spring, and it had grown back white. This meant he was revered by the clans.

Torak barely noticed the ravens. He hated leaving Renn behind. She would never forgive him. And yet he knew this had to be. His vision of the slaughtered camp could have been real. When he faced the Eagle Owl Mage, it had to be without Renn.

And without Wolf.

This was why he'd decided on an indirect route toward the Mountains. The quickest way would have been to cross the Ashwater and head southeast, following the Fastwater upstream, then on to the fells. Instead, he headed northeast up the Horseleap, toward the ridge above the river, where Wolf and Darkfur had recently moved the cubs.

To say good-bye.

The resting place was a patch of level ground on top of the cliff, bordered on one side by a fallen ash and by a bramble patch on the other. It was late afternoon when

Torak reached it, and Darkfur and the cubs gave him an ecstatic welcome; but Wolf was away hunting.

Torak was relieved. Now he would have to make a shelter and wait for his pack-brother. He could put off leaving until tomorrow.

As dusk came on, he woke a fire and built a spruce bough lean-to against the ash tree, hanging his gear out of reach of inquisitive muzzles. There were only two cubs to get under his feet. The one with the foxy ears, whom Renn had named Click, had died of a sickness the moon before.

When the shelter was finished, Torak went to pick blackberries, and the cubs came too: Shadow, the black cub with a passion for gnawing boots, and Pebble, who'd been the first to emerge from the Den and greet Torak in the summer.

The blackberries were so ripe that they fell to pieces in his hands, and the cubs snuffled them up from his palm. Shadow placed her forepaws on his knee and rose on her hind legs to give him a sticky wolf kiss, while Pebble, his muzzle stained purple, bounded off to attack the shelter. Seizing a branch in his jaws, he gave a tug that made the whole thing shudder and sent him hurtling back to his mother.

As Torak watched Darkfur licking her cubs, he knew he was doing the right thing. They were only three moons old: too small to make the trek to the Mountains.

And Wolf would never leave them behind.

Thinking of this, Torak crawled into his sleeping-sack.

It was a frosty night, and he was glad of his winter clothes: a duckskin jerkin and under-leggings, with a parka and over-leggings of warm reindeer-hide, and beaver-hide boots. He hadn't been asleep for long when he was woken by excited whimpering.

Wolf had returned. Darkfur and the cubs were lashing their tails as they gulped the meat he'd sicked up for them, while Rip and Rek sidled about looking for scraps. Darkfur was too clever for them, and the cubs had learned the hard way about raven thievery, and warded them off with growls and body slams.

In the moonlight, the resting place was spangled with frost, and the eyes of the pack shone silver. Wolf bounded over to Torak and they rolled together, nose-nudging and licking each other's muzzles. *The hunt is good, the cubs are strong!* said Wolf.

Glancing up, Torak saw that the black sky was spotted with downy white flakes.

It was the cubs' first snow, and they loved it. They chased and snapped and stalked this strange, silent prey, batting it with their paws and licking it off each other's fur. Torak knelt and they clambered over him, butting him with small, cold noses. Wolf and Darkfur joined in, and they all chased one another up the ridge and around the resting place, skittering so near the edge that they sent pebbles splashing into the Horseleap far below.

At last, Torak squatted by the fire, and the wolves lifted their muzzles and howled to the moon. Torak listened to the cubs' wavering yowls and their parents' strong, sure voices. It didn't seem possible that he could bring himself to leave. And the worst of it was that he couldn't tell Wolf, as that would only force him to make an agonizing choice: either to follow Torak and desert his family, or to stay with them and abandon his pack-brother.

Sensing Torak's unhappiness, Wolf stopped howling and trotted toward him. His thick winter pelt sparkled with snow, but his tongue was warm as he licked Torak's cheek.

You're sad, he said.

No, lied Torak.

Wolf didn't ask again, but leaned against him, comforting by his presence.

Safe with the pack, Torak slept without fear of Eostra's gray moths, and woke at dawn. The cubs lay in a snow-sprinkled huddle, with Darkfur and Wolf curled nearby.

Quietly, Torak put the fire to sleep and shouldered his gear.

Wolf's paws twitched in his dreams, but as Torak knelt beside him, he opened his eyes and stirred his tail. *You go to hunt?* he said with a tilt of his ear.

Yes, Torak replied in wolf talk. Burying his face in his pack-brother's scruff, he inhaled deep breaths of the beloved scent. Then he tore himself away.

It was a bitterly cold morning, and the snow-crust crackled under his boots. On the higher ground, the wind had exposed patches of flat bearberry scrub: the startling scarlet of spilled blood. On one patch, Torak found a dead gray moth. He touched it with his boot, and it crumbled to dust.

As he went on, he found more dead moths littering the undergrowth. The frost had put an end to them.

Or maybe, he thought uneasily, Eostra no longer needs them. Maybe they've already done their work.

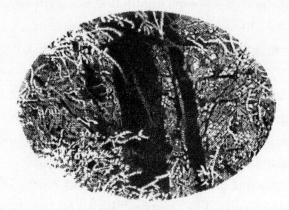

THREE

"Can't you hear them?" whispered the sick boy.

"Hear who?" said Renn.

"The demons. . . ."

Renn took a brand from the fire and showed him every corner of the Boar Clan shelter. "Aki, look. There are no demons here."

"The moths drew them," he muttered, rocking back and forth. "They'll never leave me now."

"But there's nothing—"

Grabbing her arm, he breathed in her ear. *"They're in my shadow!"*

Renn jerked back.

Aki stared about him with haunted eyes. "I hear them all the time. The clicking of their jaws. Their angry breath. In the morning when my shadow's long, I see them. At midday, when my shadow creeps closer, they're inside me. Under my skin, gnawing my souls. Ai! Get away!" He clawed at his shadow.

Renn wondered what to do. She was exhausted. For days she'd done her best to keep the gray moths from the Boar Clan, while their own Mage was laid low with fever. And now this.

Aki's fingers were bleeding as he clawed the mat. Renn tried to stop him, but he was too strong. She called for help. Aki's father ran in and clasped his son in his arms. A second man, haggard from fever, raised a spiral amulet and made the sign of the hand.

"He says there are demons in his shadow," Renn told him.

The Boar Mage nodded. "I've just seen two more with the same sickness. Renn. If it's here, it'll be with the Ravens, too. I'm well enough now. Go back to your clan."

The Boars had camped on the River Tumblerock, less than a daywalk north of the Ravens, but the fog made Renn's progress slow. As she stumbled through it, she thought of gray moths and Eostra the Masked One. Every falling leaf made her jump. She regretted having declined the Boar Clan Leader's offer to accompany her.

Her tired mind went in circles. How to stop the

gray moths? How to fight the shadow sickness? What if Saeunn was too old and weak to cope, and everything came down to her?

And like a dark current beneath it all was the gnawing anxiety about Torak.

For days she'd been reading the embers, and last night she'd placed a dream-stave under her sleeping-sack: a stick of rowan wound with a lock of his hair. Now she wished she hadn't. Everything pointed the same way. She prayed that she'd gotten it wrong.

The fog was gone by midafternoon, and she paused for a salmon cake under a beech tree. She was opening her food pouch when the zigzag tattoos on her wrists began to prickle. Quietly, she closed the pouch and examined the tree.

On the other side, someone had gouged a strange, spiky mark in the trunk. It was about a hand wide, and it had been hacked—not carved but *hacked*—into the smooth silver bark.

Renn had never seen anything like it. It resembled a huge bird with outstretched wings. Or a mountain.

And it was fresh. Tree-blood oozed from the wounds. Whoever had done this had acted from hatred and a desire to inflict pain.

Drawing her knife, Renn scanned the Forest. The light was beginning to fail. Shadows were gathering under the trees.

She knew of only one creature who could treat another with such savagery. A tokoroth. A demon in the body of a child.

She touched the scar on the back of her hand, where one had bitten her two summers before. She pictured filthy, matted hair. Vicious teeth and claws. She fancied she saw branches stir, heard a cackling laugh as the creature leaped from tree to tree.

There's nothing here, she told herself.

But she was running up the slope.

Not far now. Just over the ridge, then I'll be back in the valley of the Ashwater, and it's downhill all the way.

It was a frosty night when she reached the Raven camp. Her clan, hunched around the long-fire, greeted her with subdued nods. Nobody asked why she was frightened. Fear hung in the air. The Boar Mage was right: things were worse here too.

Two young hunters, Sialot and Poi, had fallen sick; they said there were demons in their shadows. All day they'd been gouging strange, spiky marks on everything: earth, wood, even their own flesh. Fin-Kedinn was at the river, making an offering. And Torak was gone. He'd left for the Mountains that morning.

When she heard this, Renn gave a strangled cry and rushed to her shelter.

Inside, the Raven Mage was reading the embers.

"Why didn't you stop him?" cried Renn.

Saeunn didn't look up. She sat beneath her elk-hide mantle, feeding slivers of alder bark to the fire, watching how they twisted, straining to catch the hissing of the spirits. "The Mountain of Ghosts," she breathed. "Ah . . . yes. . . ."

Renn flung down her gear and scrambled closer. "The Mountain of Ghosts. Is that the mark I found on the tree?"

"She has made her lair in the Mountain. She seeks power over the dead. Yes . . . this was always her desire."

Renn thought of Torak making his way through the Forest, not knowing what he was heading into. She started cramming salmon cakes into her food pouch.

"You would set off at night?" mocked Saeunn. "With the moths and the shadow sickness, and tokoroths waiting in the Forest?"

Renn paused. "Then at first light."

"You cannot leave. You're a Mage. You must stay and help your clan."

"You help them," retorted Renn.

"I am old," said Saeunn. "Soon I shall seek my death."

Alarmed, Renn met her flinty gaze. Even while she'd been away, the Raven Mage had declined. Beneath her mottled scalp, her skull looked as fragile as a puffball: one touch and it would collapse into dust.

But her mind remained as sharp as a raven's talons.

"When I am dead," she declared, "you will be the Raven Mage."

"No," said Renn.

"There is no choice."

"They can find someone else. It happens. People do choose Mages from other clans."

"Fool of a girl!" spat Saeunn. "I know why you shirk your duty! But do you think that even if he survived this final battle—if he vanquished the Soul-Eater and lived to tell of it—do you think he'd stay with the Ravens? He's a wanderer—it's in his marrow! You will stay, he will leave. This is how it will be!"

In that moment, Renn hated Saeunn. She wanted to shake those frail shoulders as hard as she could.

Saeunn read her thoughts and barked a laugh. "You hate me because I tell the truth! But you know it, too. You've read the signs."

"No," whispered Renn.

Saeunn grasped her wrist. "Tell Saeunn what you saw."

The Mage's claws were as light and cold as a bird's, but Renn couldn't pull away. "The—the crystal Forest shatters," she faltered.

"The shadow returns," added Saeunn.

"The white guardian wheels across the stars—"

"—but cannot save the Listener."

Renn swallowed. "The Listener lies cold on the Mountain."

"Ah . . ." breathed the Raven Mage. "The embers never lie."

"They must be wrong!" cried Renn. "I'll prove them wrong!"

"The embers never lie. Eostra will take him alone. Without you. Without the wolf."

"She *won't*!" Renn burst out. "She can't keep us apart, he won't face her alone!"

"Oh, he will. I've seen it in the embers, I've seen it in the bones, and they tell me—yes, and you know this in your heart—they tell me that the spirit walker will die!"

After a dreadful night, Renn slid into a dreamless sleep. When she woke, she was horrified to find that the morning was half gone.

The first snow had fallen, and the white glare made her blink as she emerged, thickheaded and heavy-limbed. Camp was bustling. The clan was taking down the shelters and using the saplings and reindeer-hides to make sleds, while the dogs—who knew what this meant—raced about, eager to get into harness. The Ravens were breaking camp.

Renn found Fin-Kedinn dismantling his shelter. "Where to?" she said. "And why now?"

"East, to the hills. The clans will gather there. They'll be safer near the Deep Forest." He saw her expression and stopped. "You're going after him."

"Yes." She expected him to try to stop her, but he went on with his work. His face was gray. She could see that he hadn't slept.

"Why are you breaking camp now?" she said again.

"I told you. They'll be safer near the Deep Forest."

"They? But—aren't you going with them?"

"No. Thull will lead them while I'm gone. Saeunn will counsel him when the clans gather."

"*What?*" Renn stared at him. "But—they need you more than ever! You can't leave now!"

Fin-Kedinn faced her. "Do you think I would leave my people if I wasn't convinced it was the only way? I've thought of little else for days. Now I'm sure."

"Why? Where are you going?"

He hesitated. "I need to find the one person who can help Torak. Who can help us all."

"Who's that?"

"I can't tell you, Renn."

She flinched. "You can't? Or won't?"

He didn't reply.

With a cry, Renn turned her back on him. Everything was happening too fast. First Torak. Now Fin-Kedinn.

She felt her uncle's hands on her shoulders, gently turning her around. She saw the snow sprinkling the white fur of his parka; the silver hairs threading his dark-red beard.

"Renn. Look at me. *Look at me.* I cannot tell you. Because I swore on my souls, I swore, that I would never tell."

Ice flowers grew on the banks of the River Horseleap. The trees sparkled with frost. It was too cold for the Blackthorn Moon. It didn't feel right.

Renn guessed that as Torak had decided it was too dangerous for her to go with him, he would also try to leave Wolf behind; which meant that he would go first to the resting place, to say good-bye. To save time, she crossed the river and headed up its gentler south bank. It didn't look as if Torak had done the same. At least, she didn't find any tracks.

She was too worried to be angry with him. He had lived with the burden of his destiny for three winters, and over the last summer, she had watched the dread grow. He never spoke of it, but sometimes, when they were sitting by the fire or playing with the cubs, she saw a tightening around his eyes and mouth, and knew he was thinking of what lay ahead.

If only he didn't feel that he had to do everything alone.

She'd set out so late that she wasn't even near the

resting place when she had to start looking for a campsite. She ground her teeth in frustration. Torak had a day's lead on her, and he walked fast.

A day's lead was all it would take.

FOUR

Torak had wasted the whole morning seeking a place to cross the Horseleap. The north bank had gotten steeper and steeper as he'd headed upstream, so at last he'd been forced to double back.

He was exasperated. He'd grown up in these valleys. How could he have forgotten them so quickly?

And already, he was missing Wolf. They'd been apart before, but this felt different. He almost hoped that Wolf would seek him out, and he would see that gray shadow loping toward him through the trees.

Overnight, the Forest had turned white. Torak saw drag marks where a badger had collected bracken for winter bedding; and patches where reindeer had pawed away the snow to get at the lichen beneath.

The mark on the yew tree shouted at him from ten paces away.

He wasn't sure what it meant—maybe a mountain with a great bird swooping toward it—but he sensed its intention. *I am here*, said the Eagle Owl Mage. *I am waiting.*

Torak bristled with outrage. The sign had been hacked through the bark and into the sapwood. It was as if Eostra were threatening the Forest itself.

On impulse, he shook some earthblood from his mother's medicine horn into his palm, and patted it into the tree's wounds. There. The horn was special, made from the World Spirit's antler; maybe the ochre it contained would help the yew to heal.

It was also a gesture of defiance to the Soul-Eater. *Torak did this.*

As he moved off, he heard Darkfur's distant, questioning barks: *Where—are you?* And far away, Wolf's answering howl: *Here!* They sounded happy. Torak told himself he'd done the right thing in leaving them.

But he still missed Wolf.

Wolf had slept through the Light, but as the Dark came on, he set off to hunt. He left his mate teaching the cubs to avoid auroch horns. She'd found an old one, and was tossing it up and down; the cubs were doing the rest, by leaping for it and getting biffed on the nose.

As Wolf trotted through the Forest, he caught the scents of prey gorging on nuts and mushrooms. At a spruce tree where a reindeer had scratched its head-branches, he rose on his hind legs and chewed the delicious, bloody tatters.

But some things troubled him.

It was so cold that the ground was stone beneath his pads, and even the trees were shivering. This cold felt odd. Dangerous.

And Tall Tailless was hiding something. He'd told Wolf that he was going hunting, but Wolf had sensed that he wasn't after prey. So why hadn't Tall Tailless told him? How could he hide things from his own pack-brother?

Worst of all, the Stone-Faced One had appeared to Wolf in his sleep. Through the hissing Dark she had come, and terror had seized him by the scruff. Her yowl had bitten his ears like splintered bone. Her smell was the smell of Not-Breath. Her terrible face was stiff: her eyes were not eyes but holes, and her muzzle never ever moved. As Wolf cowered before her, she had plunged her forepaw into the Bright Beast-that-Bites-Hot—*and taken it out unbitten.*

When he'd woken up, she was gone. But now, as Wolf followed the scent of a roebuck through the willowherb, he wondered if *this* was why Tall Tailless had left. Was he hunting the Stone-Faced One?

If that were true, he couldn't do it without his pack-brother. And yet—how could Wolf go with him, when he had to look after the cubs?

As Wolf was trying to get his jaws around this, a bad scent hit his nose. He caught the smells of the Stone-Faced One, and a fierce hunger to kill. And the smell of owl.

Wolf's fur stood on end.

He forgot about the roebuck and set off in pursuit.

It was the time when the light begins to turn: the clans called it the demon time.

Rip and Rek had been unsettled for a while, but Torak couldn't work out why. Maybe, like him, they were missing Renn and Wolf. Maybe it was this strange, windless cold.

Hungry, he paused on the cliffs above the river, woke up a small fire, and chewed a slip of dried horse meat. The banks were still too steep to climb down, and he'd had to backtrack almost two-thirds of the way to the resting place. He wasn't proud of himself.

He tossed a few crumbs in the ferns for Rip and Rek, but to his surprise, they ignored them. Instead, they flew to the top of a pine tree and gave long, penetrating calls: *rap-rap-rap. Intruder.*

Torak made a quick search, but found nothing.

With agitated caws, Rip and Rek flew away.

When one has ravens for companions, it's wise to heed their warnings. Drawing his knife, Torak made a second, more careful search.

At the foot of a rocky outcrop a short distance from the fire, he found an owl pellet. It was huge: longer than his hand and three times as thick as his thumb. Peering, but not wanting to touch, he saw that it was made of packed fur and bones, mostly weasel and hare. No wonder the ravens had fled. Like many creatures, they, too, feared the eagle owl.

Torak pictured the great bird alighting with its prey on the rocks above his head: ripping the carcass to shreds and gulping it down, then spewing out the pellet of bones.

Rising to his feet, he scanned the rocks above.

One moment he was gazing at mottled granite; the next, the eagle owl raised its tufted ears and hissed at him.

It was so close that he could have touched it. In one frozen heartbeat, he took in the powerful talons and the cruel, curving beak. He stared into the unblinking orange glare. He recoiled. Its pupils were black pits of nothingness. Nothing except the urge to destroy.

The owl gave a piercing cry, spread its enormous wings, and flew away, forcing Torak to duck.

He watched the owl disappear into the Forest. His

palms were clammy with sweat.

Swiftly, he put the fire back to sleep and gathered his gear.

Farther on, he found a pine marten's mangled remains. The owl had not eaten. It had killed for pleasure.

He saw one of its wing-feathers, barred with tawny and black, and coated with an unclean dust that smelled of rottenness. He'd found one just like it on the day the Soul-Eaters had taken Wolf.

That was when it hit him.

The owl had flown west.

Toward the resting place.

Toward the cubs.

FIVE

Torak couldn't reach the resting place for the brambles.

He slashed at them with his knife, he tore at them with his hands. He couldn't see what was happening, but he heard the ravens' strident caws and the snarls of a furious wolf. Darkfur was defending the cubs alone. Wolf was still out hunting.

At last Torak tore free and stumbled into the resting place. He saw Pebble cowering under a juniper bush at the edge of the cliff; Shadow lying by the ash tree at the far end: a crumpled heap of black fur. He saw Rip and Rek mobbing the eagle owl as it swooped to snatch the fallen cub. He saw Darkfur springing to the defense.

Yanking his axe from his belt, Torak raced to help her. The owl tilted its wings and soared out of reach. Torak caught a blast of fetid air as it swept back toward him. He flung up his arm. The owl struck him a dizzying blow on the forehead. As he fell to his knees, he saw it swoop with outstretched talons at Pebble's hiding-place.

Dashing the blood from his eyes, Torak struggled to his feet and ran to fend it off. He was almost there when Darkfur made a desperate leap to save her cub. The owl twisted with blinding speed, and the she-wolf's jaws clashed empty air. To Torak's horror, Darkfur landed at the very edge of the cliff. Frantically, she scrabbled. Her claws raked frozen earth. She fell.

Torak saw her hit the water far below. She went under, came up struggling. The river was too strong. She went under again.

The owl was harrying Pebble's juniper bush, the ravens beating it back. Shouting and swinging his axe, Torak threw himself into the attack. From the corner of his eye, he saw Wolf burst from the Forest and leap at the marauder. The owl wheeled, evading axe and fang and claw. It kept coming back. It had killed before and it meant to kill again.

Torak glimpsed Pebble shaking with terror beneath the juniper bush. If he stayed hidden, he had a chance, but in the open . . .

Torak barked a command, *Stay*, but at that moment, Pebble's courage broke. He bolted from his hiding-place and made for the brambles. The owl snatched him in its talons and soared into the sky.

Torak threw down his axe and unslung his quiver and bow. His fingers were slippery with blood—he couldn't get the arrow nocked.

With awesome power, the owl rose out of range, Pebble hanging limp in its talons. Mockingly, it circled. Then, in a wide, lazy arc, it turned and headed south.

Rip and Rek sped after it with raucous cries.

Wolf disappeared over the edge of the cliff.

As Torak stood swaying, he saw his pack-brother skitter down the rocks and run along the bank, frantically sniffing for his mate. Then, finding no scent, Wolf raced over a fallen pine that spanned the river, and vanished into the Forest, in a futile effort to save his cub.

SIX

The eagle owl was taunting Wolf.

Dangling the cub from its talons, it flew back to make sure that he was following, then glided out of reach. Wolf's paws scarcely touched the ground as he raced after it.

Up the rise he loped, and down into the valley where he'd had his Beginning. His claws clattered as he sped across the Bright Hard Cold that had once been the Fast Wet.

The owl swept so low that he heard the hiss of its wings. Then it rose over the treetops and disappeared.

Tirelessly Wolf ran, as only a wolf can run. But at last

he halted. The wind was at his tail, he couldn't catch the scent, and he couldn't see the Up for the trees. He could no longer hear the caws of the ravens.

Wolf felt in his fur that this time, the owl wasn't coming back.

A great emptiness opened inside him.

Darkfur was gone. The cubs were gone. *This could not be.*

The cubs were part of him. He could no more lose them than he could lose a paw. And he and Darkfur were one breath. As one wolf, they hunted in the Forest. As one wolf, they sensed which cub was planning to stray too far, and which had got stuck in the brambles. When they howled, their voices rose together into the Up.

This could not be.

Wolf lifted his muzzle and howled.

Wolf's howls drifted to Torak as he knelt on the clifftop. Such desolation. Grief without end.

Torak resolved that his pack-brother would not bear it alone. He would go after him and find some way to comfort him.

But as he got to his feet, the resting place went around and around. He touched his forehead. His fingers came away red. Better do something about that, he thought fuzzily. And yet he made no move to open his medicine pouch.

The resting place was a dismal mess of ravaged snow. Shadow lay by the ash tree, as if asleep. There was no blood. The eagle owl must have snatched her up, then dropped her from a great height. The fall had killed her instantly.

Kneeling by the corpse, Torak pictured her small souls padding about, seeking Wolf and Darkfur and her pack-brother. He longed to help her, but he didn't think wolves had death rites, or Death Marks. He'd asked Renn about that once, and she'd said that wolves don't need them. Their ears and noses are so keen that their souls always stay together and never become demons. So instead, Torak simply prayed for the guardian of all wolves to come and fetch Shadow's spirit *soon*, before she got scared.

As for her body, he carried it to the edge of the brambles and laid it on a bed of ferns. There he let it lie, with the moon and the stars wheeling over it; and in time, like all creatures, it would become food for the other inhabitants of the Forest.

It was dark. There was a ring around the moon, which meant it would get even colder. He couldn't go after Wolf tonight. He'd have to sleep here and head off at dawn.

Numbly, he collected his scattered gear and woke up a fire in front of the shelter he'd left only that morning. Then he took dried yarrow from his medicine pouch and pressed it to his forehead, bandaging it with the buckskin headband he'd worn when he was outcast.

The musty smell of yarrow reminded him of when he'd hit his head going over the waterfall, and Renn had treated his wound. He missed her. He wondered if he'd been wrong to leave the Raven camp without her. At the time, he'd been convinced he had to be on his own. But maybe that had been Eostra's trick. She wanted him alone. And now she'd made brutally sure that he stayed alone, by sending her creature to slaughter the pack and lure Wolf away.

From the south came his pack-brother's howls. Torak did not howl back. He knew the only howls Wolf wanted to hear were those he never would again.

At dawn, Torak found a precipitous way down the cliff-face and half-climbed, half-fell to the bank below.

Wolf's trail led across the pine trunk that spanned the river, but Torak did not follow it. First, he headed downstream, searching the ground beneath the cliff. Maybe—*maybe*—Darkfur hadn't been killed in the fall. Maybe she'd got ashore, and was lying battered but alive. . . .

The snow was untouched, the shallows crusted with unbroken ice.

Torak crossed the Horseleap by the pine trunk and checked the other bank. Again, nothing. Darkfur was gone.

Gone, gone, echoed Wolf's lonely howls.

Torak started along his pack-brother's trail. When the snow-crust is too hard for paw prints, a wolf leaves barely any trace—a few flakes of frost brushed off a branch, a frond of bracken bent slightly out of place—but Torak tracked Wolf almost without having to think. His trail headed south, up the side of the valley and down into the next: a rocky, steep-sided gully.

Torak recognized it at once: the valley of the Fastwater. When he was little, he and Fa used to camp there in early summer, to gather lime bark for rope making.

The river was frozen now, but three summers ago it had been a torrent. Torak recognized the big red rock shaped like a sleeping auroch. Beneath it he had found a pack of drowned wolves lying in the mud. And a small, wet, shivering cub.

Crossing the frozen river, he started to climb.

He went very still.

An arrow had been lashed with a twist of creeper to the trunk of a birch tree about ten paces above the auroch rock. It pointed east, toward the High Mountains.

Holding his breath, Torak climbed closer. He studied the fletching but didn't dare touch. The arrow had belonged to Fa.

As if his father had spoken aloud, Torak heard his voice in his mind. *Help me. Set my spirit free.*

Maybe Fin-Kedinn was right, maybe Eostra was

making use of Fa's arrow. But Torak couldn't forget that lost spirit calling in the night. If Eostra was summoning him to her Mountain lair, then so was Fa.

And yet—if he headed east, as Fa's arrow begged him to, he would be abandoning Wolf.

Torak stood irresolute, fists clenched inside his mittens. Should he follow the dead, or seek the living?

He knew what Fin-Kedinn would have done.

Facing the invisible Mountains, he lifted his head. "You tried to separate me from my pack-brother," he shouted to the Eagle Owl Mage. "Well, you won't succeed. I won't let you!"

Turning his back on his father's arrow, he headed south.

To find Wolf.

SEVEN

It turned colder and colder as Fin-Kedinn headed north.

The night before, there had been a ring around the moon, and the stars had flickered with an intensity he'd rarely seen. Storm on the way. The clan would have pitched camp early. He must do the same.

He crossed the Tumblerock at the Boar Clan camp, then made his way into the valley of the Rushwater. He was now less than a daywalk from the Windriver, where the Ravens had camped in the time of the demon bear. He thought of the day when Renn and her brother had brought in two captives: a wolf cub squirming in a buckskin bag, and a bedraggled and furious boy. . . .

The Rushwater echoed noisily between its ice-choked banks, but the Forest had a peculiar, waiting stillness. Fin-Kedinn realized that he'd seen no birds all day, save for a few last, lonely swans flying south.

And no people. The frosts had killed the gray moths, but the victims of the shadow sickness remained terrified, and their terror infected others. Most people were staying close to camp, only braving the Forest when hunger drove them.

So it was good to encounter a small Viper hunting party: three men and a boy, hurrying west to rejoin their clan. They'd caught two squirrels and three wood pigeons. It wasn't much, but they urged Fin-Kedinn to come with them and share.

"Bad weather on the way," said one. "Dangerous to be in the Forest alone." Out of respect, he didn't ask what the Leader of the Ravens was doing so far from his clan.

Fin-Kedinn declined the offer and ignored the unspoken question. Instead, he told them of the gathering of the clans.

"The Ravens have already set off, and I told the Boar Clan when I passed their camp; they'll have left by now; and Durrain has sent word throughout the Deep Forest. Go back to your people and tell your Leader. If the clans stay together, we will remain strong. Even against Eostra."

That he dared speak her name aloud gave them courage. But the hunter who had spoken grabbed Fin-Kedinn's arm. "Come with us, Fin-Kedinn. We need you. You can't leave us now."

"Others can lead," said Fin-Kedinn. "I must seek the one who can bring down the Soul-Eater. The one who knows the dark places under the earth."

"Who? Where are you going?"

"North" was all Fin-Kedinn would say.

Before they could ask more, he was on his way. Time was against him. And to find the one he sought, he must rely on knowledge many winters old.

He hadn't gone far when the boy came racing after him. "My father says to give you this," he panted, holding out a squirrel.

Fin-Kedinn thanked him and told him to keep it. The boy glanced up at him shyly. "Can I go with you? I know the land to the north—I could help you find your way."

The Raven Leader bit back a smile. He'd hunted in this part of the Forest since before this boy was born.

He was about twelve summers old, with loose limbs and a sharp, intelligent face; a little like Torak at that age. "They say you've journeyed farther than anyone," he ventured. "To the Far North and the Seal Islands and the High Mountains. Can't I come too?"

"No," said Fin-Kedinn. "Go back to your father."

As he watched the boy plodding off, Fin-Kedinn

became suddenly alert. The crunch of the boy's boots had an odd, brittle sound, which rang too sharply through the trees. And the snow looked wrong. It had an almost greenish tinge.

Fin-Kedinn's hand tightened on his staff. No wonder the Forest was bracing itself.

"Tell your father to hurry," he shouted to the boy. "Get back to camp, quick as you can!"

The boy turned. "I know! Snowstorm on the way!"

"No! *Ice storm!* Much worse! Tell your father! Run!"

Fin-Kedinn watched till the boy was safely back with the others. Then he started looking for a place to build a shelter. As he did so, he prayed to the World Spirit that Torak and Renn—wherever they were—had seen the signs too, and gotten under cover.

EIGHT

A sense of foreboding had been growing on Renn since she woke up. It was cold. Too cold for snow. The night before, there'd been a ring around the moon. Tanugeak the White Fox Mage had once told her that this meant the moon was pulling the ruff of her parka closer around her face, because bad weather was coming.

And to make matters worse, Renn had heard Wolf howling in the night. She'd never heard him howl like that before.

The River Horseleap was beginning to freeze, the shallows congealing in fragile, pale-green swirls. In an inlet, Renn found splintered ice and a trace of a paw print; farther on, boot prints, unmistakeably Torak's. She was puzzled. He'd headed *downstream*, then backtracked. Why?

Soon after, she drew level with the resting place on the other side of the river, and craned her neck at the cliff. She howled, but no wolves peered over the edge. She told herself they must have taken the cubs exploring. But her uneasiness grew.

Her spirits rose when she found the pine trunk where Torak had crossed the river. His trail was fresher than she'd dared hope, and he'd been walking with his usual long strides, so he must be all right, which meant that Wolf couldn't have been howling for him.

She followed the trail into the gully of the Fastwater. She didn't know it well, except from Torak's description of where he'd first met Wolf, but halfway up, she spotted an arrow, tied to a birch tree and pointing east. This was baffling. Torak must have put it there as a sign for her. But if he wanted her to follow, why not just wait?

For some reason, she passed the arrow without examining it, and hurried on. But to her dismay, she found no more tracks. Torak *hadn't* come this way.

She went back to the birch tree, and came to a dead stop. The arrow had been tied in place with nightshade: a deadly plant, beloved of the Soul-Eaters—especially Seshru, her mother. Torak would never have used it. This wasn't his sign. It wasn't his arrow.

A gust of wind threw back her hood. She shivered. While she'd been tracking, the wind had strengthened, and the sky had darkened ominously. Storm coming. She should make camp right now.

But then she would fall even farther behind.

Fighting a rising tide of panic, she decided to flout everything she'd ever learned, and keep going.

As the wind strengthened, she found Torak's trail and followed it into the next valley. She paused for breath under a huge, watchful holly. Her sense of wrongness deepened. It wasn't even midafternoon, but it was as dark as twilight. The snow had an odd, greenish tinge. She hadn't seen a single living creature all day.

Fin-Kedinn would have called a halt long before now. "The first rule of living," he'd told her once, "is *never* leave it too late to build a shelter."

And this was a good place for a camp: a patch of level ground near the holly tree, even if it was a bit far from the river.

Renn chewed her lip. "Torak?" she called. "Torak!"

Angrily, she flung down her gear. *Why* had he left without her? And why hadn't she caught up?

Now that she'd stopped, she realized how little time she had left.

Come on, Renn. You know what to do. First, the fire. Wake it *now*, before you're tired from chopping wood, and build the shelter around it. Plenty of tinder in your pouch, keeping warm inside your jerkin; and you've got a bit of horsehoof mushroom smoldering in a roll of bark, so no messing about with a strike-fire.

Which was just as well. The trees were moaning, and the wind was tugging at her clothes and whipping branches in her face. It was malicious. It wanted her to fail.

Gritting her teeth, she woke the fire, then wrenched her axe from her belt. Now for the shelter. Bend saplings and tie them together with willow withes, leaving a smoke-hole at the top. Build long and low to weather the storm, and cut off the saplings' heads so the wind can't pull them over—sorry, tree-spirits, you'd better find a new home. Fill in the sides with spruce boughs, plug the gaps with bracken, and weigh it down with more saplings, as many as you can.

Despite the cold, sweat ran down her sides. Too much to do, and the trees were thrashing and creaking. They sounded frightened.

Bracing herself against the wind, she wove a rough door from hazel and spruce branches, then crawled inside, dragging in firewood, and more spruce boughs for bedding. The shelter was thick with smoke, it was swirling close to the ground, too scared to leave. Coughing, Renn pulled the door shut. The smoke-hole sucked the haze upward, and the shelter cleared.

She'd made it just big enough to take two people, in

case Torak needed it too. Now she recognized that for the delusion it was. Torak was long gone.

"Water," she said out loud, trying to banish her fears. The river was too far, so she'd have to melt snow. Yanking her parka and jerkin over her head, she used the jerkin's lacings to tie its neck and sleeves shut, to form a makeshift bag. Then she pulled her parka back on and crawled out into the jaws of the storm.

The wind pelted her with flying branches and stung her face with ice needles. Quickly, she crammed snow into the jerkin, and crawled back inside. With her spare bowstring, she hung the snow sack from a support sapling, and placed a swiftly made birch-bark pail underneath to catch the drips.

The wind screamed. The shelter shuddered. Suddenly, the World Spirit speared the clouds and sent the hail hammering down. Renn hugged her knees and prayed for Torak and Wolf.

A thud shook the shelter.

She gave a start. That wasn't a branch.

Pulling up her hood, she shifted the door and peered out.

Hail struck her face.

Only it isn't hail, she thought, it's *rain*—and it's turning to ice on everything it strikes.

Screwing up her face against the onslaught, she saw the freezing rain hitting twigs, branches, trees—imprisoning all it struck in a heavy mantle of ice. Boughs bent beneath the weight. Already ice was forming on her clothes.

She groped to find whatever had fallen against the shelter. Her mitten struck a lump which didn't feel like a branch. She squeezed.

The lump squawked.

Rek's wings were clogged with ice, but once Renn got the raven inside and brushed her off, she began steaming gently in the warmth.

Shivering with terror, she cowered on Renn's lap. As Renn gazed into those deep raven eyes, she sensed in them more than terror of the storm. Where had Rek come from? Where was Torak?

A thunderclap split the sky. The Forest roared as Renn had never heard it roar before. She heard deafening cracks and tremendous, splintering crashes.

And then, quite distinctly, she heard a voice in the storm. She strained to listen. Was that—could it be Torak, calling her name?

It would be madness to go out again.

And yet—if there was a chance that Torak needed help . . .

She grabbed a brand from the fire.

The fury of the storm beat upon her. The Forest was under attack. She saw trees flailing wildly, desperate to break free of their burden of ice. Branches crashed. A pine snapped like kindling. Even the boughs of the great holly bowed so low, they threatened to split the tree in half.

"Torak!" yelled Renn. The ice storm ripped away his name like a leaf. "Torak!"

It was hopeless.

A flash of lightning, and from the holly, a face peered down at her. Icicle hair. Eyes glittering with malice.

Renn screamed.

Thunder boomed.

The tokoroth leaped into the dark.

The holly gave a groan—and tore itself apart.

Renn threw herself out of the way a heartbeat too late. One of the holly's limbs crashed across her calf, pinning her to the ground.

Wildly, she struggled, but the tree held her fast. She'd left her axe in the shelter. With her knife, she hacked at the branch. The wood was like granite; the blade bounced off. Frantically, she dug at the earth beneath her leg. Frozen hard.

Already, ice was weighing her down, sucking the life from her marrow.

"Torak!" she screamed. "Wolf!"

The wind whipped her voice away into the night.

NINE

The hill below Torak was a precarious jumble of flood-tossed logs.

He'd spent ages searching in vain for some trace of his pack-brother. And now he couldn't even get down. He guessed that Wolf had run lightly over the logs; but if he tried, he'd start a log slide.

"Fool," he muttered. A while ago, he'd passed a good campsite on some level ground near a big holly tree, but he'd been so intent on finding Wolf that he'd ignored it. The strange thing was, he'd known at the time he was making a mistake, but he'd done it anyway.

The wind tore at his hood and pelted him with

branches. The trees roared a warning: *Get under cover, fast!*

Rip thudded onto his shoulder, making him stagger. *Quork!* cawed the raven. He looked bedraggled. Torak wondered how far he and Rek had chased the eagle owl.

The raven lifted off and flew uphill.

That was the way Torak had come. Maybe Rip wanted him to get back to that campsite while he still had the chance.

Quork! Follow!

Torak followed.

The light was so bad that he could hardly see. As he crashed through the undergrowth, he glimpsed Rip's white wing-feather. Then the clouds let loose the hail.

Only it isn't hail, he thought as he ran, it's freezing rain. Torak, you're caught in an ice storm!

Bent double, he battled up the slope. He couldn't go much farther. He had to find some hollow under a boulder, anything, and wait out the storm.

He would have missed the shelter completely if Rip hadn't perched on top.

A shelter? Torak couldn't believe it. He recognized the patch of level ground, although it looked different: the holly had toppled over. And there had been no shelter here, he was sure of it.

A flash of lightning showed him the wattle door weighted shut with a stone. Thrusting it open, he threw

Rip inside and crawled after him.

With the door closed behind them, the wind's screams lessened a little, but the ice hammering the walls was deafening. The shelter was empty, but by the look of the fire, whoever had built it hadn't gone far.

And they had known what they were about. As Torak brushed the ice from his clothes, he saw that the fire had been set on a platform of sticks to keep it off the cold earth, and ringed with stones to stop it escaping. Wood was stacked on one side, while a quiver and bow hung to dry—but not too close to the flames—and a bag of snow, improvised from a jerkin, dripped water into a half-full pail.

Rip was pecking eagerly at the sleeping-sack. It moved. Rek peered out. The ravens greeted each other with much gurgling and holding of beaks. Torak's belly turned over. Why was Rek in here?

That bow. That jerkin.

Renn.

This was her shelter. Her quiver, her arrows. Over there were the crumbs of the salmon cake she'd left for Rek. And being Renn, she'd raven-proofed the rest of her food by weighting her pouch with her axe.

She'd left her weapons, which meant she couldn't have gone far.

Fear trickled down Torak's spine. In winter, you don't *need* to go far to die in a storm. Every clan has its stories of people lost in a blizzard, whose frozen corpses are later found just a few paces from camp.

Beside the wood pile, Renn had stacked some stubs for use as torches. Torak jammed one in the embers to wake it. Then, leaving his gear and the ravens inside, he seized his axe and threw himself out into the storm.

"Renn!" he yelled.

She could have been right beside him and he wouldn't have heard her.

Branches flew at him as he began to search. Doubled up against the onslaught, he circled the shelter. His torch died. He could hardly see a pace ahead.

He made another round, widening the search. Still nothing.

On his third pass, lightning flickered in the fallen holly, and through the branches he glimpsed a flash of red.

Dropping to his knees, he tore at the branches. *"Renn!"*

TEN

Renn didn't seem to be breathing. Her eyes were shut, her lips tinged blue. It was only when Torak got her into the shelter and felt her throat that he detected a tremor of life.

He shouted her name. She didn't respond. The cold had sent her deep inside herself. It would kill her if he couldn't get her warm.

Her clothes were stiff with ice. Torak pulled her parka over her head, then yanked off his own parka and jerkin. The birdskin was warm from his body; he got her into it fast. Drawing off her outer leggings, he bundled her into her sleeping-sack, checking her face, hands, and feet for the waxy flesh of frostbite but finding none.

With a stick, he rolled a hot stone from the edge of the fire and wrapped it in his empty waterskin. Then he reached inside her sleeping-sack and placed it on her belly. After that, he unrolled his own sleeping-sack and put it around her shoulders, rubbing her back, willing her to wake up.

Her eyelids flickered. She looked at him without recognition.

He dropped another hot stone in the water pail, raising a hiss of steam. Then he emptied his medicine pouch, scooped up some dried meadowsweet, and tossed it in. Tipping some of the steaming brew into his drinking cup, he held Renn's head and trickled a few drops between her lips. She spluttered. He made her drink more. She started to shiver. His dread lifted a little. Shivering was good.

The shelter was low and cramped, so he had to sit hunched, with one arm around her. As he made her drink, faint color stole into her cheeks, and her mouth lost that terrifying blue tinge. Now when she looked at him, she knew who he was.

"You're going to be all right," he told her. He needed to say it out loud. To make it true.

Her gaze took in his bandaged head. "You found me," she mumbled.

"And you built the shelter. Rip led me to it."

Hearing his name, the raven stretched his neck and fluffed his chin-feathers.

Torak did his best to scrape the ice off their parkas, laying Renn's on the other side of the fire to dry, and pulling on his own, chill and unpleasant against his bare skin. Then he shared out some salmon cakes.

Renn gave a corner to the ravens and solemnly thanked Rip for guiding Torak to her. Then she began to eat, holding her cake in both hands, like a squirrel. She was sitting up now, with the sleeves of Torak's jerkin flopping over her hands. Her face was flushed, her hair a mass of fiery tendrils. Torak felt that he could warm himself simply by her nearness.

The fire had burned low. He fed it more wood. Outside, the ice storm battered the Forest. He began to shake. The storm had nearly killed Renn. It had nearly killed Renn.

He told her he was sorry for leaving her, and she gave him an unreadable look. Then she told him how things had been after he left: about the shadow sickness, and Fin-Kedinn going off on a secret journey of his own. When Torak couldn't delay it any longer, he told her about the eagle owl attack, and the deaths of Darkfur, Shadow, and Pebble.

Renn took that in appalled silence. "All three?" she said at last.

He nodded. "I don't know how Wolf will bear it."

"All three," repeated Renn.

But she was not Fin-Kedinn's kin for nothing, and Torak could see that already she was pondering what this meant. "The owl," she said. "There must be something wrong with it."

"I saw its eyes. They were—empty."

"Ah. So not a demon."

"I don't think so."

"I wonder what Eostra did to it." Her tone was that of one Mage assessing the craft of another, and Torak admired the speed with which she'd recovered. "You say it flew south?" she said.

"Yes. It took Pebble, I think to decoy Wolf away. He's out in the storm. If he's still alive."

Renn met his eyes, and now she was more girl than Mage. "He's alive," she said. "Wolf knows how to look after himself."

Torak did not reply. In his mind, he heard his pack-brother's howls. Wolf hadn't sounded as if he cared whether he lived or died.

As Torak crouched in the flickering gloom, he fancied that amid the roaring of wind and weather, he heard wild laughter. "This storm," he said. "Eostra sent it. Didn't she?"

Renn's raven eyes gleamed. "She holds the Forest in a grip of ice."

Together they listened to the trees fall.

"After you left," said Renn, "she sent signs."

"I think I saw one. Like a spiky bird, gouged in a yew."

Renn hesitated, and he sensed her deciding what to tell him and what to keep back. She said, "The sign means that Eostra has made her lair in the Mountain of Ghosts."

The Mountain of Ghosts. Torak had never heard of it, but the name made him feel cold inside.

"Fin-Kedinn told me it's sacred to the Mountain clans," Renn went on. "He says if we can find them, they might help us find the Mountain."

With part of his mind, Torak heard her voice; but another part was thinking, there will be caves. The knowledge dropped into his heart like a stone. Twice in his life he'd ventured into caves: once in the time of the bear, to find the stone tooth, and once in the Far North, to rescue Wolf. Both times, the Walker had warned him. "Once you've gone in," the old man had said, "you'll never be whole." The Walker was mad, but now and then, he showed flashes of sanity. His warnings had force. Torak had a sudden presentiment that if he ignored them—if he ventured again into a cave—the jaws of the earth would snap shut on him forever.

Renn spoke his name, and he was back in the shelter.

"Are you all right?" she said.

"Yes," he lied.

She took his hand. Her fingers were thin and warm. He drew strength from them.

"Torak," she said. "I don't know what Eostra means to do in the Mountain. But I know this. She wants to keep you apart from me and Wolf. She wants you alone. She won't succeed."

They sat side by side while the ice storm fought the Forest with unabated fury. Presently, Renn slept, but Torak remained awake. For now, he and Renn were safe. Wolf was not. It seemed to Torak that the bond between them was a fragile thread stretching through the night— and that Eostra's icy hand was reaching out to sever it.

ELEVEN

The Bright Hard Cold was savaging the Forest. It was crushing trees and hurling birds from the Up. It was attacking Wolf with freezing claws.

Let it. He didn't care what happened to him.

He'd been running forever, casting for the scent of the eagle owl, trying to catch the least whimper from his cub. Nothing. The Bright Hard Cold had eaten hope.

He came to a hill of roaring pines where a boulder hid a small Den. Without pausing to sniff for bears, he ran in and slumped onto broken bones and ancient scat.

He knew that Tall Tailless was seeking him, but not even the thought of his pack-brother could rouse him.

Darkfur and the cubs were gone. Wolf longed to be with them—but they were Not-Breath. He didn't understand how this could be. Darkfur and the cubs were . . . *not*.

Wolf shut his eyes. He wanted to be *not* too.

Torak was woken by silence.

He was cold—the fire was half-asleep—and the shelter had sagged till it was only just above him. His breath was loud in the stillness, frosty on his face.

The door had frozen shut. He hacked it open, waking Renn, who sat up before he could warn her, and banged her head.

Bracing himself against the cold, Torak crawled out—into a piercing glare and a Forest turned to ice.

The storm had beheaded trees and transformed what remained to glittering spikes. It had flattened entire groves to mounds of twisted crystal. Tree, branch, leaf: all were caught fast in Eostra's prison of ice.

Slowly, Torak got to his feet. He took a few steps. The ice beneath his boots was hard as stone. The cold seared his lungs and crackled in his nose. The glare was a knife in his brain. Everywhere he turned, ruined trees flashed and glinted. The shattered Forest possessed a terrible beauty.

"Can you feel their souls?" Renn said behind him.

He nodded. The air shivered with the spirits of dead trees seeking new homes.

"They can't get into the saplings," said Renn. "The ice is keeping them out."

"What will they do?"

"I don't know. Let's hope the thaw comes soon."

Torak didn't think it would. A dead, windless cold lay upon the land. The hand of Eostra.

Shading his eyes with his palm, he saw a reindeer calf on the slope below. It wobbled on spindly legs, frightened by this treacherous new world, while its mother, hungry for lichen, chopped at the ground with her sharp front hooves. She couldn't break through.

Torak thought of lemmings trapped in frozen burrows; of beavers sealed inside their lodges.

He thought of Wolf.

Rip and Rek flew out of the shelter and perched on a bough, loosing a clinking cascade of shards. The echoes took a long time to die.

Renn called Torak's name, her voice shrill with alarm.

She was crouching ten paces away in the lee of a boulder, peering through the tangle of a spruce that had fallen against it. As Torak approached, she warned him back. "Wait. Don't look—"

He shouldered her aside. Between the branches, he glimpsed a patch of gray fur tipped with black. Wolf fur.

Renn was pulling his arm. He shook her off. He tore at the branches, desperate to reach—to reach what lay entombed beneath the ice.

Renn wriggled past him and got there first.

Torak's world shrank to that gray fur under the rock.

Renn's voice came to him from far away. "It isn't Wolf."

She crawled backward, clutching a band of wolfhide in her mitten.

It was about the width of a hand: rolled up, frozen stiff. "It was staked in place," she said. "We were meant to find it. It's been tanned, the edges pierced for sewing. Looks like what's left of someone's clan-creature fur."

"It is." Torak took it from her and tried to unwind it. The frozen fur cracked, and something fell out. The world tilted as Torak picked up the little seal amulet. He knew the turn of its sleek head. He'd often counted the tiny claws on its flippers. He said, "It belonged to my father."

Renn stared at him.

"His mother was Seal Clan—he always wore it." He swallowed. "He left it as a sign. He's been begging me for help. And I turned my back on him to find Wolf."

"You had to," said Renn. "Wolf needs you."

"I turned my back on Fa. That's why he left me this."

"No." Her tone was hard. "This was left by tokoroths."

"You can't know that!" he cried. "How can you possibly know that?"

"I don't, not for sure. But I know this. Eostra sent her tokoroths and her owl and the ice storm to separate us—but she *failed*. And she will fail to keep us apart from Wolf."

"And Fa?" he demanded. "What about Fa?"

She turned to the ruined Forest, then back to him. "It might not be him."

"And if it is? What then?"

"And if it is," she said, unflinching, "you were *still* right to follow Wolf. Because Wolf is alive. Your father is dead. You cannot have dealings with the dead."

Torak glared at her, but she did not back down.

"He's dead, Torak. Nothing can bring him back. Wolf needs you more."

In prickly silence they returned to the shelter, where they gathered as much firewood as they could carry, and Renn made masks of slit buckskin to shield them from the glare. Torak checked their provisions: a bag of hazelnuts, some salmon cakes, dried horse meat, and lingonberries. He wanted to take Fa's clan-creature fur, but Renn shook her head. "No, Torak. You can't take a dead man's things."

He gave in to that, but determined to keep the seal amulet. When she saw his face, she did not protest, merely insisting that he wrap it in rowan bast before putting it in his medicine pouch. He could feel her wanting to make things better between them, but he stayed stubbornly silent. She hadn't heard his father's spirit calling in the night. How could she understand?

The ice storm had obliterated all hope of a trail, but the day before, Wolf had headed south, so that was where they went. It proved almost impossible. The ice was the snow's evil sister. When they broke through frozen branches, it sent shards flying at their eyes. It made them fall, and punished them when they did. Soon they were covered in bruises.

Now and then, Torak stopped to howl. *I am seeking you, pack-brother!* The Forest threw back his howls unanswered.

At last they reached the frozen river. Torak saw the corpse of a mallard trapped in reeds, its brilliant green head carapaced in ice. He put his hands to his lips and howled.

No reply.

The river was so slippery, they had to cross it on hands and knees, but when they reached the opposite bank, they found the way blocked by a stand of fallen beech. They had no choice but to head upstream.

Torak howled till he was hoarse.

"Don't stop," said Renn. "He will hear you. He will howl back."

But Wolf did not howl back, and Torak feared that he never would. This was the valley of the Redwater, where the demon bear had killed his father. Maybe it was where Wolf, too, had met his death.

Around midafternoon, the trees thinned and a bitter wind rattled the leaves. It was the wind off the fells. They were nearing the edge of the Forest.

They came to a grove of crushed pines, and a boulder hung with icicles longer than spears.

Beneath the boulder, they found Wolf.

TWELVE

Wolf was alive—but only just.

Ice caked his fur, and his muzzle was white with frozen breath. When Torak swung his axe and sent the icicles clattering from the boulder, Wolf opened his eyes. Renn was shocked. His gaze was dull. It didn't light up when he saw his pack-brother.

Renn watched Torak crawl in beside him, trying to reassure with glance and touch and whine. Wolf's tail barely twitched.

"We've got to get him warm," said Torak, clawing ice from Wolf's pelt.

"I'll wake a fire," said Renn. "You build a shelter around us."

They worked in silence, Torak dragging fallen saplings, chipping off the ice, setting them against the boulder to close in the space; Renn rousing a smoky, reluctant blaze. In the warmth, Wolf's fur began to steam, but his eyes remained incurious, their amber light quenched.

Renn set a salmon cake by his muzzle. He ignored it. Alarmed, she tried to tempt him with a few dried lingonberries. He ignored them too. When Rip and Rek stalked in and stole them all, he didn't turn a whisker.

"Thank the Spirit we found him in time," said Torak, dragging the door shut behind him. "He'll be all right once he's warmed up."

Renn bit her lip. "Give me your medicine horn. I'll try a healing rite."

Feeling Torak watching her, she shook earthblood into her palm and daubed some on Wolf's forehead, muttering a charm.

"He'll get better now," said Torak. "Won't he? Renn?"

She did not reply. Wolf was sick to his souls with grief. And from that you can die.

As the moon rose, they got into their sleeping-sacks. Torak lay with one arm over Wolf, trying to comfort by his nearness, as in the past, Wolf had comforted him. At times, Wolf's tail stirred listlessly, but Renn could see that he was giving up.

Next day dawned icily clear, with no sign of a thaw. As light stole into the shelter, Renn saw with a clutch of terror that Wolf was no better.

Torak saw it too, but said nothing. Renn guessed that he was staring into the abyss of a future without Wolf.

Worried about their supplies, she said she would set some snares. Torak would not leave Wolf, so she went alone, not going far for fear of tokoroths. When she got back, she tried every healing rite she knew. Wolf submitted without so much as a twitch of his ears. He didn't care.

"I've done all I can," Renn said at last.

"There must be something more," said Torak.

"If there is, I don't know it."

"But he's better than when we found him. He could barely move—he's stronger now."

"Torak. You know what's happening as well as I do."

She saw the terror in his face.

"But he's still got us," he insisted. "We're part of the pack, too."

He was right. But whether that was enough to keep Wolf alive, Renn didn't know.

As dusk came on, she went to check the snares. Her hunting luck had held; one held a frozen hare. She told herself this was a good sign, but on her way back, she saw tracks. Small. Human. With claws.

At camp, she found Torak standing outside. His lips moved in silent prayer, and for one terrible moment, she thought Wolf had died. Then she saw the lock of dark hair tied to a branch. Torak was offering part of himself to the Forest in return for Wolf's life.

"Torak," she said gently, "you can't do this." She reached out to untie the offering, but Torak pushed her hand away.

"What are you doing?" he cried. "It's for Wolf!"

"I know, but *think*! Your hair contains part of your world-soul. There are tokoroths about. If they got hold of it, there's no knowing what they might do."

In furious silence he watched her untie the hair and stow it in her medicine pouch. "You think Wolf's going to die, don't you?" he said. He made it sound like a betrayal.

"If he doesn't want to live," she said in a low voice, "then no spells, or prayers, or offerings can make him."

Angrily, Torak turned his back on her.

Feeling shaky and sick, she stowed her catch in the shelter, and fed the fire, and stroked Wolf, and asked Rip and Rek to watch over him. Then she went to draw lines of power around the camp. To keep the tokoroths away.

Renn was right about Wolf, and Torak came close to hating her for it.

But what he really hated was what was happening to his pack-brother. He hated that he couldn't stop it. He hated the eagle owl. Most of all, he hated Eostra.

He slept fitfully, waking often, and always finding Wolf gazing at the fire. *I'm here, pack-brother,* Torak told him.

I miss them, Wolf replied.

I know. I'm here.

Torak sank his fingers into the warm fur of his pack-brother's chest, and felt the beat of his heart. He willed it to keep on beating.

Next time Torak wakes, it is to utter blackness. Wolf is gone. Renn is gone. He is alone.

He walks, but he can't feel the ground beneath his feet. He is cold, but he can't feel the wind in his face, or hear the creak of the trees. It is so dark that he can't see his hand when he holds it before him.

This is not spirit walking: he feels no wrenching pain. This is worse. He is still himself, Torak, but something is missing. Inside him there is a terrible, yawning emptiness.

"Renn? Wolf?" he calls, but his voice stays trapped inside his head. There is nowhere for it to go. He is alone in nothingness.

"*Renn!*" he screams as he spins in endless dark. "*Wolf!*"

Wolf woke with a start.

He heard the growls of the Bright Beast-that-Bites-Hot, and the pack-sister whiffling in her sleep. Tall Tailless was gone.

Worry gripped Wolf from nose to tail. Tall Tailless was clever, but he could hardly smell or hear, and in the Dark he was as helpless as a cub.

Swiveling his ears, Wolf caught sounds outside the Den. He heard trees shivering beneath the Bright Hard Cold, and voles scrabbling to break out of their burrows. He couldn't hear his pack-brother, but he sensed that Tall Tailless needed him.

Stepping silently over the pack-sister, Wolf left the Den. Hunger made him weak, but his senses prickled.

Lifting his muzzle, he snuffed the scents. His hackles rose as he caught the smell of demon.

Placing each paw with stalking care, Wolf moved noiselessly over the brittle ground.

Tall Tailless stood a few lopes away, beneath a spruce tree. He was swaying. His eyes were open, but he did not see, and Wolf knew that he slept.

In the tree above Tall Tailless's head, a shadow moved.

In a snap, Wolf took in everything. He saw the tailless cub-demon crouched on the branch above his pack-brother. He sensed its hunger and hatred, he saw the great stone claw in its forepaw, ready to strike.

With a snarl, Wolf sped across the Bright Hard Cold.

Something smashed into Torak and felled him.

He caught the glitter of demon eyes, the glint of a knife—then Wolf—*Wolf*—was leaping at the tokoroth, and it was scrambling up a tree and into the dark.

"Are you all right?" cried Renn, running toward him.

Dazed, he struggled to his feet. Branches cracked as the tokoroth escaped from tree to tree, and Wolf—a silver arrow in the moonlight—raced after it.

Torak tried to go after him, but his knees buckled.

"Come back inside," urged Renn.

"I've got to help Wolf."

"You're not wearing your parka. Inside before you freeze!"

Once they were in the shelter, Torak found that he was shaking, but not with cold. "Wh-at happened to me?"

"You were sleepwalking." In the firelight, Renn's face was ashen. "I woke up, you were gone. I went out, saw you standing beyond the lines of power. You looked right through me. It was horrible. I saw the tokoroth in the tree—it was aiming at your head. Then Wolf came out of nowhere. He saved you."

Torak thought of Wolf chasing the demon.

"I think Eostra made you sleepwalk," said Renn, wrenching him back.

"How?"

"I don't know. But I think she tried it once before, in the Deep Forest. Remember?"

Torak shut his eyes. That brought the blackness back, so he opened them again. "Why would she?" he mumbled.

"I think," said Renn, "she wanted to make you go beyond the earthblood I'd laid down, so that her tokoroth could get you. But *why*?" she said to herself. "It wouldn't make sense to kill you, then your power would be lost. It doesn't fit. None of it fits."

Torak rested his forehead on his knees. Renn touched his cheek with the back of her hand and asked how he was feeling, and he said all right. She asked how he'd felt when he was sleepwalking, and he said, "Empty. I was in nothingness. I was lost."

Renn sucked in her breath. Torak asked her what it meant, but she wouldn't say. He knew she was keeping things from him. He didn't care. Wolf had saved him, and now he was out there alone. Against the tokoroth.

The demon disappeared into a thicket, and Wolf lost the scent. Shaking himself in disgust, he turned and trotted back to the Den.

The Bright Hard Cold bit his pads, and he was extremely hungry and weak; but he felt better than he had since the owl attacked, and he held his tail high. He had saved his pack-brother from the demon. This was what he was for.

As he neared the Den, the ravens swooped and croaked at him, and he made a feeble play-leap to chase them away. The ravens were *with* the pack, but not *of* it; they had to be kept in their place.

The pack-sister came out of the Den and said something surprised in tailless talk. Then she ducked inside and came out again, with her forepaws full of those small, flat salmon that didn't have any eyes. Wolf gulped the lot, and felt much better. He was licking the last bits off her paws when Tall Tailless came out of the Den. Tall Tailless saw Wolf and went still. Wolf gave a whimper and threw himself at his pack-brother, and they rolled, whining and rubbing their noses in each other's delicious scent.

The Hot Bright Eye rose in the Up, splashing the Forest with light, and Wolf felt that this was good. Darkfur and the cubs were gone, and he would miss them always; but he understood now that he couldn't be with them. Tall Tailless and the pack-sister were part of the pack, too, and they needed him.

A wolf does not abandon his pack.

THIRTEEN

The wolf cub did not *at all* understand what was going on.

How had he got to this empty hillside so far from the resting place? *And where was the pack?*

He remembered the ravens cawing, and the terrible owl attacking his mother. He'd watched them fighting from under the juniper bush: his mother leaping and snapping, the great owl lashing out with its claws. Then his mother wasn't there anymore, and his father was fighting the owl, and Tall Tailless was barking at the cub to *stay*, but he couldn't. He fled, and suddenly claws were biting his flanks and he couldn't feel the ground, he was *flying*.

He'd wriggled and whined, but nobody heard him. His father and Tall Tailless shrank to dots as the terrible owl carried him higher. Even the ravens dropped behind. Then there was no more Forest, only empty whiteness speckled with sticks that looked like trees.

The cub had whimpered in terror.

The owl flew for an endless time. Next thing, the cub woke to angry caws, and the ravens were diving out of the Up. They were mobbing the owl, who was twisting and swerving. The cub tried to bite its legs, but he couldn't reach. Again and again the ravens attacked. Suddenly the owl let go and the cub was falling.

He plopped into the Bright Soft Cold and lay shaking, too frightened to move.

When nothing happened, he struggled upright and poked out his head.

The terrible owl was gone.

So was everything else. No ravens. No Forest. No wolves. Only the wind and the white.

Digging himself out of the Bright Soft Cold, the cub floundered uphill to sniff the smells, as he'd seen his father do. His flanks hurt and his legs shook. He was hungry and very, very scared. He put up his muzzle and howled.

Nobody came.

The cub had eaten some of the Bright Soft Cold, but though it filled him up a bit, it didn't chase away the hunger.

Wearily, he padded along the hillside. The wind had dropped and the Dark was coming. His claws felt strangely tight, and he sensed that everything—the hill, the Bright Soft Cold, even the Up—was waiting: for something bad.

He came to a clump of small, twisted willows that clung to the slope. They reminded him of the resting place, so he decided to stay close.

Nosing around, he found what seemed to be a Den. From it came an interesting smell that he couldn't remember.

Just then, something hit him on the nose. With a yelp, he sprang back—and something hit him on the rump. Now it was pelting him all over, hitting his back, ears, paws. It was coming from the Up. He raised his head. It hit him in the eye. He shot under a willow.

The pattering grew to a thunder. The Bright Hard Cold was roaring from the Up, snapping branches, pummeling the cub.

The Den. Get inside the Den.

Seizing his courage in his jaws, he made a dash for it.

Ha! The Bright Hard Cold couldn't get him in here! He heard it snarling, furious at not being able to reach him.

The Den was only a bit bigger than he was, but at the back, that interesting smell was much stronger. The cub remembered it now. *Wolverine.*

Wolverines are extremely fierce, but luckily, this one wasn't moving. The cub sniffed. He extended a wary paw. The wolverine was Not-Breath.

The cub was used to eating soft, chewable meat which his mother and father sicked up; he had to struggle to get his jaws around a part of the wolverine. The meat was so tough, it was like chewing a log, but after much gnawing, he tore off a chunk and gulped it down.

He ate till his jaws ached and his belly felt full. Then he rolled in the rotten smell and went to sleep.

When he woke up, the Bright Hard Cold was still pounding the hillside, so he ate some more wolverine and slept. And woke. Ate. Slept. . . .

When he woke again, all was quiet.

In the Now that he'd gone to in his sleep, he and his pack-sister had been clambering over his mother, play-biting her tail while she nuzzled their bellies.

In *this* Now, he was alone.

He whimpered. The noise he made in the stillness frightened him, so he stopped, and gnawed some more wolverine. Then he padded to the mouth of the Den.

The glare hurt his eyes. No smells. The only sounds were a strange crackling, and the hissing of the wind.

Blinking, he saw that the willows lay broken beneath

the Bright Hard Cold. The whole world lay beneath the Bright Hard Cold.

He ventured out. His paws shot from under him and he fell. He scrambled upright, digging in his claws.

Above him rose the white hill. Below him it swooped down, then up again. The cub didn't dare move. There was nowhere to move *to*. He lifted his muzzle and howled.

It was the strongest, least wobbly howl he'd ever managed—but no wolf answered.

Instead, a raven flew down, landing a few lopes away from him. Then another.

The cub lashed his tail and yowled with joy. These were *his* ravens, they belonged to the pack! Sleeking back his ears, he bounded toward them, slithering about on the Bright Hard Cold.

The ravens flew off, laughing. The cub didn't care, he was used to their tricks: they often pecked his tail and stole his meat. He raced after them—forgot about digging in his claws—and slid down the hill.

Still cawing with laughter, the ravens flew after him.

Crossly, the cub got up and shook himself.

The ravens lifted into the sky and flew away.

He barked. *Come back!*

The ravens circled over him, then flew off again, waggling their tails as they disappeared over the hill. *Quork! Follow!*

The cub labored after them. When he reached the top of the hill, what he saw made him whimper in terror.

Above him rose the biggest rocks he'd ever seen; far bigger than even the boulder beyond the resting place.

Quork! croaked the ravens.

The cub was terrified. But he didn't want to get left behind.

Narrowing his eyes against the wind, he started after the ravens, toward the Mountains.

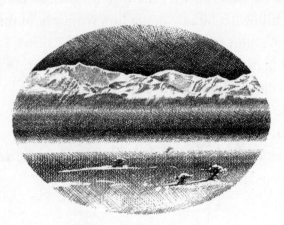

FOURTEEN

"How many daywalks to the Mountains?" said Torak.

Renn shook her head.

They stood with the Forest at their back, staring over the rolling, snowbound fells. Far in the distance—yet dreadfully present—rose the shining peaks of the High Mountains.

Torak's spirit quailed. From where he stood, he made out thousands of tiny pinnacles. Any one could be the Mountain of Ghosts. And his only hope of finding it lay with the Mountain clans.

Renn seemed to hear his thoughts. "The reindeer will

be heading for the shelter of the Forest. Fin-Kedinn says the Mountain clans always follow the reindeer. If we're lucky, we'll meet them."

Torak didn't reply. He wanted to crawl into the Forest and hide.

Wolf came to lean against him. Torak slipped off his mitten and sank his fingers into his scruff. Wolf licked his wrist: a brief flash of warmth, snatched away by the wind.

"And remember," said Renn, "she *wants* you to find her."

"But not you," said Torak. "And not Wolf, or Rip and Rek."

"She tried to separate us. She failed."

"She'll try again."

Together they stared across the fells. A howling wind sent spears of snow streaming toward them. *Go back, go back!*

The ravens *loved* it. They swooped and soared in the fierce, cold, empty sky. Rek spun somersaults, while Rip folded his wings and plummeted onto a rise, landing in a puff of snow, flipping onto his back, and rolling down the slope. At the bottom he shook his wings, flew to the top, and started all over again.

Wolf gave a *wuff!* and bounded after him, but Rip hopped onto the wind and lifted out of reach. Wolf stood on the rise lashing his tail, gazing down at Torak. His fluffy pelt was spangled with snow, and his eyes were bright. *Let's go!* he yipped.

Their eagerness gave Torak courage. He turned to Renn. "I think we can do this."

She opened her mouth to protest.

"All we've got to do," he said, "is find the reindeer."

She pointed at the fells. "How?"

"We've got a wolf, two ravens, your Magecraft, and my tracking skills. We'll find them."

They didn't.

For three days they labored over the fells without seeing a single hoof print. The flat white light made it impossible to judge distances, and the Mountains got no closer, while the fells proved even more formidable than they'd looked. They were seamed with gullies, frozen lakes, and iced-up thickets, some chest-high, others only ankle-deep, but always forcing them into a zigzag course. In places, they floundered through snowdrifts, while on ridges, the wind had blown away the snow to the pebbly ice beneath.

They tried to keep east, steering by the sun and the stars, but clouds defeated them, and they were led astray by what looked like reindeer, and turned out to be boulders.

They survived because of what they'd learned in the Far North. They wore masks against the glare, and rubbed their faces with Renn's marrowfat salve to prevent windburn. They dug snow holes for shelter, and snared a ptarmigan and ate it raw, saving whatever twiggy firewood they could gather for melting ice. They kept their gear inside the snow hole so it wouldn't get lost in a drift, and their waterskins in their sleeping-sacks, to stop them from freezing. Nights were cold. They dreamed of stacks of beautiful, dry wood.

On the third day, they spotted people in the distance, and hurried to meet them—only to find a man made of turf. He was bearded with icicles and his outstretched arms were antlers, supported by a spear in either hand. He didn't feel threatening, just oddly welcoming.

"Some kind of guardian?" said Renn. "Maybe the Rowan Clan's—they build their shelters out of turf."

"Then they made him last autumn," said Torak. "There's moss on those antlers." He scanned the fells. The Forest was long gone. All he could see were white hills. Beneath his boots, snow hid the ice which sealed off the land. Eostra had not relaxed her grip. And she was watching him.

"Dusk soon," said Renn. "We need to stop."

They camped under the gaze of the turf man, in the lee of a hill by a frozen lake ringed with scrub. Renn said she would dig a snow hole, then try a finding charm for the Mountain clans. Torak went to set fishing lines and snares. Their supplies were down to a handful of hazelnuts, and so far they'd only caught a single ptarmigan.

Wolf trotted off to hunt, followed by Rip and Rek, who clearly thought he had a better chance than Torak.

On the lake, Torak hacked holes with his axe, then fed in juniper hooks on pine-root twine he'd brought from the Forest. To stop the holes from refreezing in the night, he plugged them with twigs and covered them with snow. Then he planted his knife beside them to deter Rip and Rek, who were quite capable of hauling in the lines with their beaks, and stealing the catch.

Back on shore, he circled the lake. The land felt empty, but his hunter's eye told him it was not. He spotted splayed wing prints where a gray owl had punched into the snow after a lemming. Farther on, a cluster of shallow hollows, each with a tiny pile of frozen droppings, where willow grouse had huddled together for company. And a web of ptarmigan prints, although no sign of their beds; ptarmigans like to fly high, then dive into soft snow to make a snug, invisible burrow.

They also love birch twigs, so Torak broke off some ankle-high branches of dwarf birch, rubbed off the ice, and stuck them in a patch of snow to make a tempting cluster, in which he hid snares of looped twine. He did the same with willow for the grouse.

Farther up the slope, he found a hare trail. Following it to a windy ridge, he set his snare just before the point where the hare would have to leave the safety of the scrub and cross open ground. It would be preoccupied, and so less likely to notice a snare.

By now, Torak was giddy with hunger. All that awaited him at camp was his share of the hazelnuts. The sky was a deep, cold blue, strewn with stars. The moon was not yet up, but he made out the fanged blackness of the Mountains—and above them, faint and far, the red star of winter. The eye of the Great Auroch.

When the red eye is highest, Fa had said as he lay dying, *the demons are strongest.*

The Eagle Owl Mage and her minions were vivid in Torak's mind; but Fa's face was a blur. With a shock, Torak realized that he'd become a different person since his father had died. Maybe Fa wouldn't even recognize him. Maybe that was why his spirit had fled from him at the Raven camp.

"Fa," he said into the dark. "It's me. Torak. Where are you? How do I find you?"

The only answer was the hiss of windblown snow.

Huddled in her sleeping-sack, Renn listened to the whispering snow.

She was hungry and tired, but she knew she wouldn't sleep. The finding charm had been worse than a failure. A wall of ice had slammed shut in her mind. *Turn back,* commanded the Eagle Owl Mage. *None can hinder Eostra.*

Renn had been left dazed, clutching her pounding head. She felt so bad that when Torak returned, she had to ask him to sprinkle the earthblood around their snow hole. It wasn't a line of power, only a Mage could do that, but it was better than nothing. And maybe the turf man would help keep the tokoroths away.

Curled on her side, Renn watched the sky through the slit in the snow hole, and tried to work out Eostra's purpose.

The Eagle Owl Mage wanted Torak's spirit walking power, that much was clear. But how did she mean to take it? And when?

Torak crawled into the shelter, and Renn heard him take off his boots, pat them down for a pillow, and get into his sleeping-sack. He asked if she felt better, and she said no, and he said he was sorry. A few moments later, his breathing changed. Like a wolf, he had the knack of falling asleep in an instant.

Around middle-night, the half-eaten moon rose, and Renn asked it for help. She'd always felt close to the moon. She was sorry when the sky bear ate it, and she took strength from the fact that it always came back.

The moon.

Renn started awake. Why didn't I see it before? *I've been ignoring the moon!*

In several days, it would be the dark of the moon. And this moon was special: Souls' Night, when the

World Spirit turns from a stag-headed man to a woman with red willow hair. A dangerous time, when ghosts are abroad, seeking the clans they have lost. When the dead get closest to the living.

Souls' Night.

This was what Eostra was waiting for. With a clutch of dread, Renn saw how it fitted with what she and Saeunn had foreseen. The Listener shall die. . . .

Until now, she had pushed that to the back of her mind. But soon, Torak would have to be told.

Sitting up, she saw that he was deeply asleep, frowning in his dreams. These days, he slept as if he didn't want to wake up.

It isn't fair, thought Renn. Why does he have to be the Listener? Why does he have to be different?

Turning on his side, Torak burrowed into his sleeping-sack, his hair falling over his face.

I'll tell him soon, Renn decided. But not yet.

Besides. A dark night on the fells was a bad time to talk of prophecies; and that line of earthblood around the camp was fragile. There was no knowing what might be listening.

FIFTEEN

Fin-Kedinn watched the pine marten dart up the tree. Then he moved on, careful and silent. The one he sought might be listening.

For days he had searched the places where his quarry used to hunt long ago. On the fringes of the Deep Forest, the Lynx Clan had heard rumors; the Bat Clan had found traces which had brought him south again, to this gully. And all the time, Torak and Renn were out there alone against the might of Eostra.

In the gully, nothing stirred. A while ago, these rocks would have echoed with the chatter of water, but the ice storm had silenced the stream with a blast of freezing breath. Now each ripple would last the whole winter. That wave cresting the boulder must wait till spring to fall.

Fin-Kedinn reached a fork in the trail. One path wound west, the other east, deeper into the hills. There were no tracks. He had to rely on the Forest to guide him, and on what he knew of the one he sought.

He took a few paces up the first trail. A woodpecker alighted on a pine trunk, cocked its scarlet head, and peered at him. *Kik! Kik!* Then it flew away.

He heard a distant clicking as a squirrel scampered from branch to branch. Farther along, he found a small pile of droppings on a tree stump: twisted, musky smelling. Pine marten, perhaps the one he'd just seen.

Too many inhabitants on this trail. It probably wasn't the one.

Retracing his steps, he started up the other trail. Around him, spruce trees were frozen white cones. Under one, an auroch had cracked the ice with its hoof to get at a clump of willowherb.

In itself, this told Fin-Kedinn little, but among the remains of the willowherb, he found an exposed pine root which had been only partly stripped of bark. On it lay a brittle brown hair. He guessed that after the auroch had left, a red deer had come along and nibbled the bark; but it hadn't had the chance to eat it all. Its tracks were deep and splayed as it fled up the trail. Something had frightened it.

Not a bear; they were asleep for the winter. Lynx? Wolf? Fin-Kedinn didn't think so. He'd seen no yellow scent-markings in the snow, no claw-marks on trees. Perhaps, he thought, a lone hunter had caused the deer to flee.

Dusk was falling. Soon the first early stars would appear, although the half-eaten moon would not rise until middle-night. Fin-Kedinn hadn't gone far when he paused to listen. In the distance, a jay's warning call. A moment later, the dry swish of wings as it flew overhead, saw him, and gave another rattling *kshaach!*

It had been higher up the ridge when it uttered its first cry; Fin-Kedinn guessed that whatever it had spotted was near the top. He knew these hills. Ahead lay a rocky overhang: a good place to hide and keep an eye on what approached. And if he was wrong, he could shelter there for the night.

As he climbed, he caught a whiff of woodsmoke.

He heard the crack of a branch. Or was it the crackle of a fire?

Moving behind a holly tree, he scanned his surroundings.

Ah. Clever. Nowhere near the overhang, but down in that dell, thirty paces off the trail. The fire was hidden behind a boulder, and cast only the faintest glow. Fin-Kedinn hadn't expected less. The one he sought knew how to hide.

Quietly, he descended into the dell.

In the gloom, he made out a shadow that wasn't a rock. It sat hunched over the remains of a small deer, with an axe near to hand.

Fin-Kedinn loosened his knife in its sheath and took a step closer. Stopped. Went on again.

The shadow rose, snatched the axe, and swung at him.

Fin-Kedinn gripped the axe-arm by the wrist.

Face to face, they strained against each other.

Abruptly, the tension went out of the axe-arm.

Fin-Kedinn relaxed his hold. "Time to make amends, old friend."

SIXTEEN

The fish-hooks came up empty, and a wolverine had raided the snares in the night.

"So no daymeal," said Torak, flinging down the lines.

Renn blinked at the empty hooks. "We'll have to eat lichen."

He threw her a doubtful look. "Can people eat that?"

"I think so." But she didn't sound too sure.

Torak helped her scrape a few handfuls from under the ice, and they put them to soak in her waterskin. While she fed the fire, he went foraging. After a long, cold search, all he'd managed were a few crowberries and some frost-bitten sorrel.

Renn added them to the cooking-skin, where the lichen had stewed to a dark, slimy sludge.

"Are you sure people can eat this?" said Torak after the first mouthful.

"The Mountain clans do. If times are bad."

"They'd have to be bad. Very bad."

"Maybe Wolf will have better luck. We could share some of his."

Torak didn't relish the idea of scavenging one of Wolf's kills, but Renn was right. It had been two days since their last ptarmigan. It was now vital to find the reindeer: not only to find the Mountain clans, but to eat.

By midmorning, they reached a river which, surprisingly, was still awake. It rushed noisily between stony hills crowned with three more of the strange turf men. Its shallows were free of ice. Torak and Renn grubbed up clumps of brilliant green horsetails, and munched the swollen root-buds raw.

As he straightened up, Torak's head whirled. The horsetails had done little to assuage his hunger. His belly was beginning to hurt.

Renn slumped on a rock and took off her mask. Her eyes were ringed with blue shadows. "You'd think there'd be fish in it," she said. "But I haven't seen any."

They glanced at each other. How long could they go on?

"When we find the reindeer," said Torak, "I'm going to eat a whole one. Starting at the neck and working my way down. I'll kill another one for you."

She smiled wanly.

He squatted to refill his waterskin. "What river is this, anyway?"

"I don't know and I don't care. If I don't get meat soon, I'll eat my medicine pouch."

But Torak had stopped listening. Whipping off his mitten, he plucked something from the water.

"What is it?" said Renn.

He showed her: a light-brown hair, as long as his thumb.

Reindeer.

"They must be upstream," said Renn.

They listened. The river was too loud.

Its banks were boulder-strewn and impassable. They'd have to make a lengthy detour around the hills, or climb them. They decided to climb. It would be quicker, and give them a better view of whatever lay on the other side.

Climbing proved harder than they expected. Torak was appalled at how weak he'd become. Black spots swam before his eyes, and every step was an effort. Beside him, Renn's breath came in gasps.

Wolf appeared above them, pausing beside a turf man before racing down to Torak. His fur was fluffed up with excitement. *Reindeer! Hurry! We hunt!*

Torak translated for Renn.

Behind her snow mask, her eyes gleamed. "Let's go."

Swiftly, Torak told his pack-brother in wolf talk that he must hunt without them, as he'd have a better chance of making a kill. Wolf didn't argue, and disappeared over the hill.

The thrill of the hunt gave Torak and Renn new strength. As they neared the top of the hill, they dropped to the ground and belly-crawled. Reindeer have keen senses. If there were any on the other side, it was vital not to spook them.

Slipping his bow from his shoulder, Torak took an arrow from his quiver. Renn had already done so. She'd also tied back her red hair and tucked it inside her hood, so the prey wouldn't see. Catching his eye, she touched her clan-creature feathers and gave him her familiar, sharp-toothed grin.

The wind chilled Torak's face. Good. It was blowing his scent away from the prey.

Stealthily, he crawled forward. He crested the ridge. He caught his breath.

Below him the hill fell away to the glittering sweep of the river. *Another* river flowed across it: a river of reindeer. Clouds of frosty breath hazed golden in the sun from thousands of muzzles. The air rang with the bleating of calves and the grunts of their mothers; the nasal hoots of rutting bucks. And beneath it all, like the beating of a great heart, the steady drumming of thousands of hooves.

Torak had only ever seen small groups of reindeer in the Forest. Awestruck, he watched the herd flowing slowly, purposefully, endlessly across the river. The hill where he lay dropped steeply through a thicket of willows to a flat expanse of gravelly riverbank, then rose again to another hill, also thick with willows. He guessed that the gap in between was one of the reindeer's ancient crossing places. Fin-Kedinn had once told him that the herds have followed the trails of their ancestors for thousands of winters.

He saw how they converged in a dense press of bodies as they passed through the gap. He saw the lifted heads and jostling antlers of swimming reindeer, the quick heave as they climbed the banks and scattered on the other side. He knew that this river of life would be trailed by many hunters: eagles, wolves, ravens, wolverines, people.

But where *were* the people?

He spotted Rip and Rek flying high, turning their heads from side to side as they searched for carcasses. He saw a buck rise on its hind legs and run a few paces to warn the others of danger, then thud to earth and charge a wolverine, which bounded away. And there in the distance was Wolf, a gray shadow at the edge of the herd, seeking an abandoned calf, or a reindeer too sick or injured to put up a fight.

But no people. Just three more turf men on the hill opposite, standing with antler arms outstretched.

Renn whispered in his ear. "We're out of arrowshot. We've got to get downhill, into the thicket."

She was right. Forget about people. The only thing that mattered now was meat.

And they'd have to get close. Success in a reindeer hunt depends on making a swift kill which fells the prey quietly, without alerting the herd. If you miss, they'll be off, and you'll have lost your chance.

Renn muttered a prayer to her guardian, and Torak asked the Forest to bring him luck. They began to edge down the slope toward the willows.

Torak glimpsed Wolf weaving among the reindeer. In his head, he wished him good hunting.

Wolf ran through the rich, swirling scent that made his pelt tighten with hunger.

He smelled the bloody tatters that swung from the reindeers' head-branches, and snuffed the delicious scent of calves. To his relief, he smelled no other wolves: no stranger pack which would attack a lone wolf who dared enter its range.

To make the prey run, he let them see him.

A big bull put down his head and thundered toward

him: *Get away from my females!* Wolf dodged the lunging head-branches and bounded away.

In the din, he caught an anguished bleating. He loped toward it.

The calf stood shivering on a small, pebbly island in the middle of the Fast Wet. Wolf smelled its fear. It was unprotected. Its mother lay dead, her carcass already picked clean.

Wolf lowered his head and moved down the bank and into the Wet. He swam with the reindeer, and they ignored him, sensing that he wasn't after them.

The calf smelled him. Its bleating turned shrill. Wolf saw it move behind its mother's rib cage, ducking its head so that it couldn't see him, but sticking out its pale, fluffy rump.

Wolf's paws touched pebbles. He'd reached the island.

But as he emerged, a big cow reindeer surged onto the other side of the island and charged at him. Wolf scrambled to avoid her. She threw down her head and lashed out with her head-branches. Wolf leaped. The head-branches missed by a whisker, spraying him with pebbles. He'd made a mistake. That carcass wasn't the mother. *This* was. Wolf shot past her and jumped into the Wet.

As he reached the safety of the bank, he glanced back. The calf had ducked under its mother's belly to suckle, but the mother was still glaring at Wolf: *Stay away!*

Shaking the Wet from his fur, he scanned the herd for easier prey.

He caught a distant bleat of pain. There. A young buck struggling to climb the bank. Its head-branches looked sharp as fangs: one swipe would gut an unwary wolf.

But there was something wrong with its leg.

SEVENTEEN

Torak spotted Wolf among the reindeer, then lost him again.

Renn whispered in his ear: "These willows are too thick, I can't get a clean shot."

He nodded. "If we can get down to those rocks by the river . . ."

Silently, they threaded their way between the man-high trees on the slope. Through the branches, Torak glimpsed reindeer trotting over open ground toward the water. They ran as reindeer do, with muzzles raised and hind legs splayed, white rumps swaying from side to side.

Beside him, Renn had taken off her snow mask. Her

eyes shone. He knew she was thinking of marrowfat, and baked haunch so succulent that when you bite it, the blood squelches between your teeth and runs down your chin. . . .

Stop it, Torak. You haven't got one yet.

As it was still the rut, bulls kept turning aside to clash antlers, scattering cows and calves as they raced after each other. The biggest bulls had swollen necks and heavy manes from throat to knees; some bore bloody tatters on their tines, where the hide hadn't finished peeling. Torak saw shreds of it fluttering from branches at the edges of the thickets on either side of the gap. The reindeer shied from these, as they did from the turf men who stood with open arms on the hills and banks.

Almost, thought Torak, as if they were herding the prey.

He noticed that the reindeer weren't as plump as they should be. After grazing all summer, they should have had thick pads of fat on their backs, but these didn't. Torak saw a young cow drop to one side and make a pitiful attempt to feed, pawing the ice with her front hooves, before trotting wearily on.

At last, he and Renn made it down the slope to an outcrop of boulders on the riverbank, surrounded by straggling willows. Torak saw reindeer jostling to get into the water. He saw moist pink tongues sliding over yellow teeth. He smelled musk, and heard the clicking of tendons as hooves struck icy ground. He nocked an arrow to his bow.

Renn pushed back her hood, fixed her eyes on her target, and took aim.

Wolf bit hard and the buck with the broken leg went limp.

In a frenzy of hunger, Wolf sank his teeth into its belly and loosed a flood of delicious, slithery guts. He gulped them fast, leaving only the pouch that smelled of moss. When the buck's belly was empty and Wolf's nearly full, he started on the haunches, biting off chunks of hot, juicy meat.

The ravens alighted and hopped toward the kill. Wolf growled them away without lifting his muzzle. They stalked off to wait their turn.

The hunger was gone: Wolf couldn't eat any more. He was thirsty. His muzzle and chest fur were sticky. Trotting down the bank, he snapped up the Wet, leaving the kill to the ravens.

As he raised his head from the Wet, he caught the scent of taillesses. He sniffed.

Not *his* taillesses.

Other.

Renn was about to shoot when her quarry stumbled in the shallows, and fell with a spear quivering in its ribs.

A *spear.*

Torak met her startled glance and lowered his bow. Where had that come from?

The spear had dropped the reindeer so cleanly that the others splashed past it, unconcerned. Crouching among the willows, Torak and Renn peered down the bank. Those spears had come from the river. . . .

There. Midstream, in the thick of the herd: a hide canoe. Torak saw a wooden reindeer head at the front, a stubby tail at the back. The craft sat low in the water, manned by hunters he could barely see. He made out four, cunningly disguised: antlers strapped to their heads, faces painted dark brown, with patches of white around eyes and mouth, like reindeer. He saw another canoe downstream. Renn pointed to two more upstream.

Torak glanced at the shreds of antler hide fluttering at the edges of the thicket; at the turf men with open arms. They were there to herd the reindeer toward the river, where the hunters lay in wait, ready to pick them off while they were swimming, and least able to escape.

Renn had grasped it too. "Now we've done it," she breathed. "We've blundered into someone else's hunt!"

Torak saw a hunter in one of the boats taking aim at a white reindeer in the water. Just as his spear drew back, a raven swooped out of nowhere.

"Oh, no," muttered Renn.

Rip had eaten well, and was in the mood for fun.

Flying low, he barked like a dog. The startled hunter cast his weapon, but missed his quarry's ribs and struck the rump instead. The white reindeer scrambled out of the river and galloped off, trailing the spear.

In an instant, the herd smelled the pain of its wounded sister and panicked. Torak saw white-rimmed eyes and flaring nostrils. Panic became a stampede. Reindeer reared, clambering over one another, churning water. The canoes rocked wildly; Torak saw hunters clinging on. Then he forgot about them as branches snapped behind him and reindeer crashed toward them through the thicket.

"Climb the boulders!" cried Renn.

They fled the willows and Torak boosted her onto the nearest rock, then swung himself up. The herd thundered around them, a torrent of antlers and hooves and powerful, crushing bodies. Renn wasn't high enough—the tine of a rearing bull snagged her hair. She screamed, struggling one-handed to pull free. Torak whipped out his knife and slashed her hair loose. The terrified bull thrashed its head and flailed its hooves, catching him on the shoulder. He fell, rolling sideways as a hoof struck the ground near his face. Renn leaned down and grabbed his arm. The reindeer blundered down the bank.

"You all right?" Renn shouted above the din.

"Yes! You?" yelled Torak.

She nodded grimly. But the back of her scalp was

bleeding, where a lock of hair had been torn out by the roots.

Suddenly it was all over. The last reindeer cantered down the bank. The hoofbeats faded. The herd was gone.

Renn slid off the boulder, clutching her head. Torak jumped down beside her.

Below them, the hunters were splashing into the shallows, dragging their canoes. Already, some were running into the thicket, jabbing their spears as they sought those who'd ruined their hunt. Torak saw scowls on painted faces, heard voices buzzing like angry wasps. They had a right to be angry. One reindeer down and another wounded—which would mean tracking it, maybe for days, to finish it off. Not much of a catch for such a big clan.

Renn yanked him back behind the boulders. "We need to get away before they see us," she hissed.

"But they're our only chance of finding the Mountain."

"Yes, but right now, they're furious, and in no mood to give us directions!"

The hunter who'd been the victim of Rip's prank was the angriest. "Did you see it?" he shouted. "A demon like a raven! Spoiled my aim, then vanished into thin air!"

Torak was about to call out, but Renn clapped her

hand over his mouth. "Are you mad?" she whispered.

Torak studied the hunters. Then he took Renn's hand from his mouth, rose to his feet, and stepped out from behind the rocks.

EIGHTEEN

Renn saw a big man turn and narrow his eyes.

"Krukoslik!" shouted Torak, tearing off his snow mask and running down the bank.

The painted face split into a grin. *"Torak!"* Striding forward, the Leader of the Mountain Hare Clan put both fists to his chest in friendship. "You've grown tall! Is that Renn over there? Come down, come down!"

Embarassed at not having recognized him, Renn did as he said, and everyone crowded around. Most were Mountain Hare, but Renn also saw a few rowanbark necklets and swan feathers tied to hoods. All had broad faces and welcoming smiles. Their anger seemed to have burned off like mist.

Torak tried to apologize for spoiling the hunt, but Krukoslik waved that away. "There's another crossing place at the next river, more hunters waiting. Come! You look hungry."

Someone had already woken a fire. Krukoslik thanked the fallen reindeer for its body, and wished its spirit a safe journey to the Mountain. Then three men swiftly skinned it. After emptying the stomachs, they swilled one clean and drained the blood into it, piled the innards and stomach contents on the hide, and quartered the carcass. Nothing was wasted, and the snow was barely reddened.

Their deft work reminded Renn of Fin-Kedinn, and she felt a pang of homesickness. She was also shaky from her encounter with the reindeer, and her scalp throbbed. A Rowan woman saw her touching it, and quietly helped her bind on a sorrel poultice, which slightly numbed the pain.

Krukoslik handed Renn and Torak beakers and urged them to drink. The blood was turning stringy as it cooled, and Renn coughed when she gulped it down; but the reindeer's strength quickly became hers, and she felt a bit steadier.

Krukoslik's son Chelko—the young hunter who'd missed his aim—passed them chunks of raw liver: warm and unbelievably delicious. Now Renn felt *much* better.

She mumbled a belated thanks to her guardian, as she'd forgotten before.

Krukoslik sat with them, but ate nothing. He'd scrubbed off his paint, revealing a round face that looked permanently flushed, as if by a good fire. Like the rest of his clan, he wore a calf-length tunic of reindeer fur, tied at the waist with a wide scarlet belt. His brown hair was cut short across the brow to reveal his red zigzag clan-tattoo, and his hare-fur cape was also stained red, although it had been turned inside out for the hunt.

His eyes were shrewd, yet kind. When Renn unknowingly flouted the custom of his clan by turning her back on the fire, he gently corrected her. "We don't do that—the fire doesn't like it."

But he was also Clan Leader, used to doing things his way. When Torak asked about the Mountain of Ghosts, he stopped him. "This isn't the place. You will come to our camp, while Chelko tracks the wounded one. Then we'll talk of sacred things."

Torak nodded, and turned to Chelko. "I'm sorry the raven startled you. You should know that he's—sort of our friend."

Chelko blinked. "Your friend?"

"He didn't mean any harm," said Renn. "He's young, he likes tricks."

Chelko scratched his chin and grinned. "And I thought it was a demon."

"So it's really our fault," said Torak, "that your hunt was spoiled. I'd better help you track the wounded one."

Chelko looked pleased.

"Good," said Krukoslik. "This is good."

"I'll go with you," said Renn.

But to her surprise, Torak shook his head. "You're still shaken. You should go with Krukoslik."

"I'm fine!" she protested.

"I'll see you at camp," said Torak.

Krukoslik's small eyes darted from one to the other. "Good," he said again. "Torak goes with Chelko, Renn with me. When we're together again and everyone's eaten, you can tell me why you've come."

Renn wasn't looking forward to a long walk to camp, but she needn't have worried. The hunters had kept their dog sleds away from the reindeer, but at a whistle they arrived, driven by the children entrusted to mind them.

The sleds were of antlers lashed with willow withes, the runners coated in frozen mud rubbed smooth. They were smaller than those of the Far North, with just enough room for one person to sit, while the driver stood behind. First, Krukoslik introduced Renn to each of his dogs. He clearly thought they merited the same courtesies as people, which made her like him even more.

They started north, rattling over the icy ground. Krukoslik didn't use a whip; he called commands to his lead dog, who did the rest. While he drove, he made Renn tell him the news from the Forest. He frowned and touched his clan-creature skin when she spoke of the moths and the shadow sickness, and he was troubled that Fin-Kedinn had gone off on his own; but he seemed glad that Wolf had come with them, although he asked Renn not to name him out loud.

"We who live in the eye of the Mountain are careful with names. The gray one who is your pack-brother, we call his kind ghost hunter, because they stalk with such skill. And we don't name the prey aloud, either, as they have keen ears, and might hear our hunting plans. We call them the antlered ones."

His face creased with worry. "It's good that you've brought the ghost hunter. For three moons, none of his kind have been seen or heard on the fells—except for a dead one, which some Rowan hunters found in the west. They put food by its muzzle to feed its souls, then left it in peace. We fear the others have fled because"—he lowered his voice—"because of the evil one."

Renn glanced over her shoulder. The jagged peaks were suddenly much nearer.

Krukoslik did not speak again, and they went on in silence. The shadows were darkening to violet as they reached camp. From a distance, it looked tiny, nestled beside a gray lake in the immensity of the fells. As they drew closer, Renn saw many shelters honeycombed with golden light: the huge hide tent of the Mountain Hares, the turf domes of the Rowans, and long mounds banked with snow, which Krukoslik said were Swan.

"These are terrible times," he said. "The Mountain clans must stay together. It's our only chance."

The dogs barked as the sleds slewed to a halt, and shafts of gold speared the snow as hunters emerged to greet them. Krukoslik handed Renn a bone blade for brushing the snow from her clothes. Stiff with cold, she followed him inside.

She was greeted by a blast of heat and a wonderful, smoky smell of hot food and people. A large peat fire glowed in a ring of stones. Around it, on reindeer pelts flung over layers of springy birch, men and women sat sewing or grinding spearheads. Steam wafted from cooking-skins. Renn's hunger came back in a rush.

Taking off her outer clothes and hanging them to dry on a cross-beam, she followed Krukoslik around the fire, careful not to turn her back on it. Those she passed nodded to her with wary friendliness, but she felt conspicuous, and wished Torak were here.

Krukoslik settled himself at one end of the shelter. "Nearest the Mountain," he said as she sat beside him. He thanked the fire and the antlered ones for the food, and everyone did the same, while Renn mumbled a prayer to her guardian. Then the eating began.

A woman handed Renn a bowl, and explained that

the stew was mostly fat: crushed marrow and back fat, tongue, and the fattiest innards.

"Meat is good," said the woman, "but fat's better when you live on the fells."

Renn found the stew strengthening, but the fat stuck to the roof of her mouth, and she had to wash it down with heather tea. After that there was reindeer paunch stuffed with chewed lichen—this she politely declined— and platters of ribs and chewy, roasted ears. The toddlers had bowls of reindeer-foot jelly, and a mother gave her teething baby a stick of frozen marrow to gnaw. The elders got the reindeer's eyeballs, and nibbled the fat off them before popping them in their mouths and munching them whole.

Krukoslik apologized that there were no berries. "Because of the ice," he said. It was the only time he mentioned it.

When Renn was full, she curled up and lay listening to the sound of the fire and the murmur of voices. She was exhausted—she could still feel the movement of the sled bumping over the ice—but for the first time in days, she felt safe. Outside, the fells lay in Eostra's grip. In here, it was almost possible to forget.

Drowsily, she heard the creak of the tent poles, and the snow blowing against the shelter. In the smoky half-darkness, she watched naked toddlers clamber over their elders, who steered them clear of the fire without glancing up from their work. The Mountain clans lived with more uncertainty than most; maybe that was why they took such pleasure in the good things.

And yet, Renn saw the hardships they endured. Some were missing an eye from encounters with antlers. Others had lost fingers to frostbite. Krukoslik had said that his people didn't name their children till they reached their eighth summer, in case they fell sick and had to be left to die.

Thinking of that, Renn fell asleep.

She woke to shouting and laughter. Torak and Chelko were back.

Chelko beamed as he told everyone how Torak had summoned the ghost hunter, who'd helped them track the wounded reindeer. "I killed it with a single spear-cast. Then some Rowans came by with their sleds and helped us."

The clan looked at Torak with cautious respect, and a woman took a reindeer head outside as a present for Wolf.

Torak spotted Renn and came to sit beside her, bringing with him the clean, cold smell of the night. As he gulped a bowl of stew, he asked if she was feeling better.

"Of course I am," she said tartly.

He warded off an imaginary blow.

Around them, talk sank to a murmur, and children

snuggled into their sleeping-sacks. The Mages of all three clans came in and began to circle, mouthing spells.

"To keep us safe," murmured one of them to Renn. She wore a necklet of white feathers, and her clan-tattoo was a ring of thirteen red dots on her forehead, for the thirteen moons of every cycle. Her eyes were pale, as if bleached by staring into great distances, and with a swan's thighbone she blew earthblood on the walls, breathing life into images of the guardians. A hare sat up on its hind legs and scanned for danger. A swan glided on wide wings. A tree spread protecting arms. There were spirals, too, and reindeer, and bisonlike creatures with downward-curving horns.

Renn shivered. The Swan Mage had reminded her that only the thickness of a reindeer-hide stood between them and the dark.

Torak sat with his arms about his knees, watching sparks shooting up the smoke-hole.

Suddenly, Renn felt the distance between them of things unsaid. She knew he had secrets from her. When he'd emptied his medicine pouch during the ice storm, she'd seen a scrap of the black root that made him spirit walk. He must have gotten it from Saeunn. And he hadn't told her.

But that paled beside what she hadn't told him.

"Renn," he said quietly. "Do you remember your dreams?"

"What?" she said, startled.

"Your dreams. When you wake up. Can you remember them?"

"Mostly. Why?"

"Since we left the Forest, I can't. It's all just black. What does that mean?"

She swallowed. Tell him, tell him.

At that moment, a strange, booming groan echoed through the night.

Krukoslik saw them jump. "It's the lake. It's freezing. Crying to the Mountain to send more snow to keep it warm. We need this too. An end to this accursed ice that's starving the antlered ones."

Firelight leaped in Torak's eyes. "The Mountain," he said. "It's time for you to tell us what you know."

NINETEEN

K rukoslik laid more peat on the fire, releasing a bitter tang of earth.

Renn glanced from him to Torak. In the red gloom, their faces were shadowed and unfamiliar.

"We who live at the edge of the world," said Krukoslik, "call two mountains sacred. The Mountain of the North, which is home to the World Spirit, and the Mountain of the South: the Mountain of Ghosts. But no matter how far we hunt from the Mountain of Ghosts, it's mother and father to us. It makes the rivers and the snow. It holds up the sky. It sends the sun, the bringer of all life. It takes the spirits of the antlered ones and gives them new bodies. And it shelters our ghosts, the souls of the dead who have lost their way."

Renn said softly, "Souls' Night. What happens on Souls' Night?"

"Souls' Night?" Torak turned to her. "You think that's what she's waiting for?"

She signed him to silence.

"On Souls' Night," said Krukoslik, "the Mountain gives up its dead. When the wind howls, we hear them: the thundering hooves of the antlered spirits, and the lonely cries of the hungry ghosts." His face softened. "We comfort them. We put out piles of lichen for the antlered spirits, and for our ghosts we build a shelter. We fill it with warm clothes, their favorite foods, toys for the young ones. And a fire to banish the dark."

He smiled. "Oh, it's a good time! For a day and a night we keep them company, singing songs, telling stories. Then it ends, as it must, and we send them from us. Many of them find their way to peace"—he pointed to the smoke-hole—"and join the ancestors, hunting the great herds which trek across the sky. Others don't, and go back to the Mountain. But they'll try again next winter, and we'll help them. We'll never let them down."

Torak said what Renn was thinking. "But this winter . . ."

Krukoslik's face darkened. He reached out and touched one of the painted guardians. "It began the spring before last. We lost children. They vanished without trace. Dog sleds went missing. The wreckage turned up far away. Then the moths came, and the shadow sickness. Yes, Renn, we've had them too. Now ice starves the antlered ones. And yet it was less than a moon ago that our Mages began to suspect where the evil one had made her lair."

"But what does she *want*?" said Renn. "What will happen on Souls' Night?"

"No one knows," said Krukoslik. "Terrible cries have been heard in the foothills. Small, owl-eyed demons have been glimpsed flitting among the stones. Our Mages see visions: the gray terror gnawing the innards of the Mountain." He swallowed. "We fear that she has taken it for her own. This—this was always her way."

"You *knew* her?" said Torak.

"Even the evil one was young once. When I was a boy, some of the Eagle Owl Clan still lived. Good people. We used to see them at clan meets. Eostra was different. Hungry for the secrets of the dead." He glanced about him. The Mages had moved on to another shelter; everyone else was asleep. "It's said," he went on, "that when she became a Mage, she carried out the forbidden rite."

Renn gasped. "She did that?"

"What?" said Torak. "What did she do?"

Krukoslik leaned forward. "One of her clan had been killed in a rockfall: a boy of ten summers. They say that on Souls' Night, in the moon's dark, she went to the cairn where the body lay. To raise the dead . . ."

Renn put her hand to her clan-creature feathers. She shut her eyes. She saw a windswept hillside, a tall woman with long dark hair standing before a cairn.

The cairn heaves. Rocks fall away. Eostra peels back her sleeve and draws her knife across her forearm, anointing the lifeless flesh with blood. The dead boy sits up. His head turns. His clouded eyes meet hers. From his mouth bubbles the froth of decay. Like a lover, Eostra stoops. Her long hair caresses his face as she brings her head close, close—as she licks the corpse-froth from his moldering lips. . . .

With a start, Renn opened her eyes. Torak's hand was on her shoulder. "Renn," he whispered.

She wiped her mouth with her hand.

Krukoslik was scowling at the fire. "She'd got what she wanted," he said. "Henceforth, she could talk to them. Soon after, sickness took the rest of her clan. And Eostra disappeared."

"And joined the Soul-Eaters," said Torak.

"She *became* a Soul-Eater," said Krukoslik with peculiar intensity. "This is what you must understand, Torak. People say the Soul-Eaters took that name merely to frighten, but with Eostra, it's true."

"What do you mean?" said Renn.

"The Swan Clan frequents the high passes.

Sometimes they venture near the Gorge of the Hidden People. They've seen her. They say she walks with a three-pronged spear for snaring souls. They say that if you hear her cry, you're lost."

Lost. . . . Renn's fingers tightened on her clan-creature feathers.

"That cry," said Krukoslik, "rips the souls from your marrow. With her spear she snares them. She *devours* them. Eostra truly is an eater of souls."

Torak placed his hands on his knees. "But I have to find her," he said.

Renn shot him a glance. "You said 'I.' Not 'we.'"

He didn't reply.

Krukoslik was shaking his head. "They say this is your destiny, Torak. But after what I've told you—"

"Krukoslik. Three winters ago, in the time of the bear, you helped me find a Mountain. Will you help me now?"

"This is no small thing you ask," said Krukoslik. "Our Mages used to go into the Mountain, but not anymore. There's only one way to reach it, and that's secret."

"You have to tell me."

They faced each other, while the wind moaned and the lake cried out to the Mountain.

Krukoslik sat straighter. Once again, he was the Clan Leader who must be obeyed. "We'll sleep now. I'll give you my answer in the morning."

Renn woke to an unnatural silence that made her skin crawl.

The fire burned, but it made no sound. The walls of the shelter heaved in and out, but she couldn't hear them, or the moaning of the wind. Torak turned his head and muttered in his sleep. His lips moved noiselessly.

Slowly, Renn sat up.

At the far end of the shelter, in the dark of the doorway, someone stood.

Renn's heart began to pound.

The figure was tall. Its back was turned toward her. She saw ashen hair hanging in lank coils. From the shadowy head rose the spiked ears of an eagle owl.

Renn wanted to wake Torak, but she couldn't move. Her hands lay in her lap like stones.

The figure in the doorway must *not* turn around. If it did—if it faced her—her heart would stop.

Slowly, the figure turned.

TWENTY

Eostra the Masked One, whom even the other Soul-Eaters had feared. Her carved mouth gaped on darkness. Her unblinking glare froze Renn's souls with dread.

A dead chill settled on the shelter. The fire sank to ash. Ice crusted the reindeer-hides and the faces of the sleepers. Renn's breath smoked.

Beside her, Torak slept with one arm flung above his head. Frost spiked his eyelashes and glittered on his skin. His lips were white.

Renn spoke his name. He didn't stir. She cried it

aloud. Only a wisp of frosty breath showed that he was still alive.

"They hear nothing," said a voice like the rattle of bones. "They know nothing. Eostra wills it so."

"You're not real," said Renn.

"What Eostra wills shall be. Eostra commands the unquiet dead. Eostra rules Mountain and Forest, Ice and Sea." Her voice was barren of emotion. The Eagle Owl Mage was dead to all feeling save the hunger for power.

Renn told herself that she, too, was a Mage. She started to speak a charm of sending, to banish this evil from the shelter.

The Masked One never moved, but Renn felt icy fingers on her throat, choking off the spell.

"None may hinder Eostra."

"You're not real!" gasped Renn. "I'm not afraid of you!"

"All fear Eostra." Slowly, the feathered arms rose, and their shadows took wing. In an instant, the Masked One stood by the dead fire, looming over Renn.

Torak lay between them. Renn saw the unclean robe pooling about him. She saw the pulse beating in his throat. Exposed. Vulnerable.

"You can't have him," she said.

The terrible mask leaned toward her, unbearably close. Ashen hair slithered across her cheek. She caught the stench of rottenness.

"The spirit walker," said Eostra, *"is already lost."*

Renn stared into the pitiless, painted glare. Horror tightened its coils. Hope fled.

With a cry, she tore her gaze away. She saw the Soul-Eater's hand clenched on the head of a mace. Her flesh had the grainy density of granite; her talons were tinged blue, like those of a corpse. Between the fingers bled a fiery glow. The fire-opal.

"His time draws near," said the Masked One.

Terror hooked Renn's heart and jerked it like a fish. "You can't know that for sure."

"Eostra knows all. He cannot escape." One feathered arm reached out and she raked the ruins of the fire. She opened her talons. Ash fine as crumbled bones hissed down onto Torak's unprotected face: filling his mouth, covering his eyes.

"No," said Renn.

"Eostra shall suck the power from his marrow. She shall devour his world-soul and spew what remains into endless night."

"No!"

"From host to host, her souls shall spirit walk down the ages. Eostra shall conquer death. All shall cower before the undying one. *Eostra shall live forever!*"

"No!" screamed Renn. *"No no no no no!"*

Men shouted. Dogs barked. The shelter was in an uproar.

"Renn!" Torak was bending over her. "Wake up!"

She went on screaming. "No! You can't have him!"

The eagle owl glared down at her from the rim of the smoke-hole. Then it spread its wings and lifted into the dark.

"Was it a vision?" said Torak. "Renn? Was it one of your visions?"

"She was real."

"But she wasn't here, in the shelter."

"She was."

They sat with their backs against the peat-pile: Renn rigidly clutching her knees, Torak with one arm around her shoulders. Krukoslik had gone to the Swan Clan shelter to talk with their Leader. Most of the men were outside, calming the dogs. On the other side of the fire, women soothed children and cast fearful glances at Renn.

She'd stopped shaking, but she felt drained, as she always did after a vision. This had been the strongest and the worst ever. Dully, she stared at the glowing embers. No trace of the ash which Eostra had poured over Torak like a death rite.

"Tell me what you saw," he said in a voice so low no one else could hear.

Haltingly, she told him: about Eostra planning to rule the unquiet dead, and become the spirit walker. "She means to eat your world-soul. That's where your power lies. She will eat it and—and spit out the rest. Then she'll be the spirit walker. She'll move from body to body. She'll live forever."

"And I'll be dead."

She turned to him. "No. That's the worst of it. You wouldn't die. You'd be Lost."

"Lost? What's that?"

She sucked in her breath. "It's when you lose your world-soul. You're still you—name-soul and clan-soul—but you've snapped your link with the rest of the world. You're adrift in the dark beyond the stars, in the night that has no end. Eternally alive. Eternally alone."

In the fire, peat smoked and spat.

Torak withdrew his arm and leaned forward so that she couldn't see his face. "When I was sleepwalking, I felt lost in nothingness. You were shaken when I told you. That's why, isn't it?"

She nodded.

"But why did I feel it then?"

"I don't know. Maybe she was trying out a spell. I don't know."

He pushed the hair from his face, and she saw his hand shake. "Can it happen to anyone? Or am I more at risk?"

"I think—you're more at risk. Because you're the spirit walker. And . . ." She hesitated. "Because you broke your oath."

He waited for her to go on.

"When you swore to avenge the Seal Clan boy, you took your oath on your knife, your medicine horn, and your three souls. When you broke that oath, it may have weakened the link between them."

He was silent, staring at the fire.

"But Torak," Renn said fiercely. "All this is only what Eostra *wants*, not what has to be! We won't let it happen. We can fight it together!"

Torak gave her a look she couldn't read.

Then daylight was flooding the doorway, and Krukoslik was stamping snow off his boots and letting in the dawn.

"It's decided," he said. "We'll take you to the Gorge of the Hidden People, but no farther. You'll have to find your own way in."

TWENTY-ONE

Torak had no time to take in what Renn had told him. The camp sprang into action, people running to harness dogs and prepare the sleds.

He and Renn were hustled off and given clothes "fit for the Mountain." When Torak got outside, the sky was overcast, and the peaks were hidden from sight. But he felt them as a tightness in his chest.

Renn emerged, looking ill at ease in her new clothes. They each now wore an inner jerkin and leggings of diverbird hide, the plumage warm against their skin; a calf-length tunic of supple reindeer fur, cinched at the waist with a broad buckskin belt; socks and undermittens of soft, light woven stuff which the Swans said was musk-ox wool; and long boots and overmittens of tough reindeer forehead skin.

Such clothes must have taken days to make. When Torak remarked on this, Renn gave him an odd look. "Can't you guess? These were made for Souls' Night. They've given us clothes for ghosts."

Krukoslik came over to them. His face was grim—his camp had been menaced by a Soul-Eater—and he would not be going with them. A party of Swans would take them as far as they dared.

Krukoslik introduced their Leader, Juksakai, a slight man with disconcerting pale-blue eyes and a permanent frown. With a jerk of his head, he indicated that Renn would go on his son's sled, Torak on his. Torak thanked him for helping them, but Juksakai only scowled and shook his head.

As Torak got on the sled, Krukoslik said, "I wish you'd change your mind, Torak."

"You think I'm going to fail," Torak replied.

"I think you're brave. But foolish. Such people don't live long in the Mountains. I hope I'm wrong." Touching his clan-creature skin, he stepped back from the sled. "Good-bye, Torak. And may your guardian run with you."

Juksakai shouted a command to his dogs, and they were off.

All day they rattled over the ice, climbing first into the foothills and then the Mountains themselves, which remained shrouded in cloud. For a while, Rip and Rek flew alongside Torak, but they were soon off again, as if summoned away. Torak saw no sign of Wolf. He wondered if his pack-brother had caught the scent of the eagle owl, and given chase.

The wind was bitter. The lowering clouds weighed on Torak's spirits. He thought of being Lost in the dark beyond the stars. "Eternally alive," Renn had said. "Eternally alone."

They camped in a stony hollow where the invisible Mountains loomed over them. This was as far as the sleds could go. Tomorrow they would continue on foot.

The Swans built shelters by propping the sleds together and draping them with hides weighted with rocks. There were no trees, but fires were swiftly woken. Torak asked how, and Juksakai showed him a heathery plant which burned even when wet. He also showed Torak the cloven tracks of musk oxen, and clots of fine wool snagged on scrub. "Be warned. They're faster than bison and can scale slopes you can't. And they're the prey of the Hidden People; we only ever gather the wool."

The Swans were good at ice fishing, and a frozen lake yielded a pile of burbot and char. Over nightmeal, Juksakai thawed a little. He told Torak and Renn how his clan hunted in the Mountains with slingshots, and he showed them his clan-creature skin, a plaited wristband of swanhide, dyed red. The Swans, he said, used their clan-creature sparingly: children wore the claws, men the skin, women the feathers, the Leader the beak.

After they'd eaten, he insisted that Torak and Renn take what he called a steam bath, sitting with hides draped over their heads, dripping water onto hot stones and breathing in the steam. The Swans took no part in this, but watched in unnerving silence.

When it was over, Torak asked Juksakai why his clan was helping them.

"We're not," he said. "We're helping us."

"What do you mean?" Renn said uneasily.

The Swan Leader regarded Torak. "You seek the Soul-Eater in the Mountain. Maybe when she has you, she will send a thaw, and the antlered ones can eat."

Torak grasped the significance of the steam bath: a ritual purification. He gave a wry smile. "So I'm a sacrifice."

Juksakai did not reply.

Renn looked stricken.

The dogs were restless in the night, and Torak slept badly. Renn, too, appeared tired; and she wouldn't meet his eyes. Torak felt the tension between them. He'd known for a while that she was keeping something from him. He wondered when she would have the courage to tell him.

Another overcast day, and the Mountains stayed hidden. The Swans led them through a snowy pass that followed a rushing river upstream. The ground rose so steeply that Torak and Renn had to use their hands to climb. Breathless, they lagged behind.

The Swans pitched camp by the river, at the mouth of a deep ravine. Two shelters were swiftly built by stretching hides over existing walls of stone and peat: the remains of Mages' shelters, said Juksakai.

Renn slumped on a rock and put her head on her knees.

Torak took deep breaths, but still felt breathless. "What's wrong with us?" he panted.

"We're getting near the sky," said Juksakai. "Less air. Spirits don't need to breathe." Nervously, he fingered his wristband. "This is as far as we go. Tomorrow you're on your own."

Renn sat up. "You mean . . ."

Juksakai nodded. "The Gorge of the Hidden People."

Torak took a few steps toward the ravine. Precipitous cliffs reared above him, overhung by strange, twisted crags like enormous creatures peering down. A rocky trail wound inward, following the river. Cloud seeped from the Gorge, shielding the Mountain from view—but Torak felt its icy breath. He saw the Swans muttering prayers; Renn touching the clan-creature feathers tied around her waist.

After a silent nightmeal, Juksakai took a portion of fish, made a reverent bow to the river, and cast the fish in the water. "This is one of the veins of the Mountain," he explained.

Torak asked its name, and Juksakai replied sternly that it was never spoken aloud. "But I think you in the Forest call it the Redwater."

"The Redwater?" Torak was startled.

"You know it?"

"I—yes. It was near the Redwater that my father died."

Leaving Juksakai, he climbed down the bank and stared at the foaming water. This felt like an omen: the past thrusting into the present, like old bones emerging after a thaw.

An eerie twilight bathed the camp. As Torak turned to face the Gorge, the clouds parted—and at last there it was: the Mountain of Ghosts. Distant still, yet it towered above him. Snow streamed from its single, perfect peak which held up the sky. Its white flanks seemed lit from within by its own sacred light.

For three summers, Torak had pursued his quest against the Soul-Eaters over Sea and Ice, Forest and Lake—and it had brought him here. In a flash, he perceived that on those far-off slopes, he would meet his destiny. And for him, nothing lay beyond. On the Mountain, he would die.

This was what Renn had been keeping from him. This was the dread which had been growing inside him.

Panic flared. Run. Let someone else fight Eostra. You never asked for this.

But what about Fa?

The thought dropped into his mind like a pebble in a pool. In some way that he couldn't yet fathom, his father's spirit was linked to this: his final quest against the last of the Soul-Eaters. He couldn't turn his back on Fa.

As he stood craning his neck at the Mountain, a great loneliness opened up inside him. He needed Wolf.

Putting his hands to his lips, he howled for his pack-brother.

The echoes wound into the Gorge of the Hidden People: fainter and fainter, dying to silence.

After a time, something howled back.

It wasn't Wolf.

Juksakai ran to him, his pale eyes bulging with fear. "What was that?"

"I don't know," said Torak. He scanned the darkening campsite. "Juksakai," he said sharply. "Where's Renn?"

TWENTY-TWO

What was *that*? thought Renn.

Not Wolf. Not even *a* wolf. A dog? No dog sounded like that. Thank the Spirit it was so far off.

Hurriedly, she pulled up her leggings.

It had been dusk when she'd left, but now she could hardly see the sides of the gully. Night comes fast in the Blackthorn Moon. She should've remembered that.

With a flicker of irritation, she realized that she was going the wrong way. Those huge slabs of rock aslant each other: she hadn't seen them before.

Scowling, she retraced her steps. Stupid to have gone such a distance from camp, she'd only needed to get downstream and out of sight. The Swans had warned her to mark her trail if she went off on her own. "Easy to get lost in the Mountains, especially for a girl from the Forest." She hadn't thought it necessary. Now it looked like she was going to prove them right.

She wasn't frightened. It wasn't completely dark, and camp had to be close. It was just that Torak would tease her, and she'd rather not give him the chance.

Hurrying out of the gully, she slipped on a patch of black ice and nearly fell. She decided to give him the chance. "Torak!" she called.

No reply.

"Come on, Torak, this isn't funny! I need to know where you are!"

No answer. Only the stealthy hiss of wind. The brooding watchfulness of stones.

Uneasily, Renn remembered that the Swans had pitched camp by the noisy river. Torak wouldn't be able to hear her.

And like a fool, she hadn't told anyone where she was going.

Another howl shattered the stillness. Much closer than before.

The hairs on her arms stood up. She listened to the echoes die.

An answering howl, ending in two short barks. A signal. She ran, scrambling over mounds of loose scree.

This had to be the way back.

Dead end.

Stumbling, she headed out. Her mittens slipped off her hands and flapped on their strings like trapped birds. Her breath sounded panicky and loud.

Darkness closed in. She halted to listen.

No howls; no terse, signaling barks. That was worse. Whatever hunted her was coming on in silence, as hunters do.

She ran into a wall of rock. Craning her neck, she saw the glitter of stars. She felt the red glare of the Great Auroch. Horror washed over her. What had Eostra created?

A trickle of pebbles.

Straining to pierce the blackness, she made out sheer slopes on either side. She was back in the gully. Around her, shadow shapes shifted and came together.

High above, something detached itself from the dark. Renn sensed rather than saw it raise its head and snuff the air.

She fled, leaping over rocks, careening off boulders. The stones watched her go.

Her foot jammed in a crack and she fell, pain exploding in her ankle. She couldn't run, couldn't put weight on it.

Behind her, she heard the click of claws.

Hide. It's your only chance.

She groped, found a gap, and crawled in, dragging her

injured foot. She scrabbled for something to block the hole. She couldn't find anything bigger than her fist.

She'd have to leave her hiding-place. She couldn't. *She could not do it.*

Pebbles rattled as the creature raced down the gully.

Crawling out, Renn fumbled for a rock. Found one, too heavy to lift; half-rolled, half-dragged it toward the hiding-place. The creature was so close, she heard its sawing breath.

One mitten on its string snagged under the rock. Sobbing with terror, she yanked it free, squeezed into the hole, hauled the rock after her, pulling it *tight*, shutting herself in.

Something smashed against it. The force shuddered through her. She clung to the rock, her only defense. She felt a gap where it didn't fit. Three fingers wide. It felt like a ravine.

Outside, silence.

Sweat poured down her spine.

Through the gap, breath scorched her fingers. Whimpering, she withdrew her hands as far as she dared.

A growl reverberated through the rocks. Renn screwed her eyes shut. The growl subsided to panting breath.

Now came the scratching of powerful claws. The creature was digging her out.

She smelled its stink. She sensed its limitless hunger

to destroy. It would drag her screaming from the hole. It would sink in its fangs and rip out her throat as she lay twitching, still alive.

She couldn't breathe. But she would rather suffocate than face what was outside.

As she pressed deeper into the hole, her knife jutted against her hip. Awkwardly, she drew it from its sheath. When the creature came for her, she might be able to ram the blade into its jaws. She might make a brave death, even if there was no one to see it.

Abruptly, the digging ceased.

Renn opened her eyes.

She heard a wet smack of jaws, as if the creature had jerked up its head. Then the whisper of pads on stone, receding fast.

Could it really be moving away?

Renn bit down on her lower lip. Stay here. It's a feint. It's got to be.

It wasn't. The creature was gone.

Renn was still cowering in her hiding-place when she heard voices, and Torak calling her name.

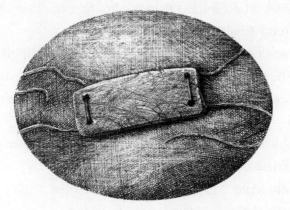

TWENTY-THREE

"I can't say for sure what it was," said Renn as they helped her into the shelter, "but I think . . ." She winced as her injured foot touched the ground.

"I saw a shadow like a huge dog," said Torak. "Then it was gone. As if someone had summoned it."

"I didn't hear anyone calling," said Juksakai.

"You wouldn't," said Torak. He described the grouse-bone whistle he'd once made for summoning Wolf. "It didn't make any noise, but Wolf could hear it. If what attacked Renn is anything like a dog, then it can hear what we can't."

Renn sat shivering by the fire. The other Swan hunters

were staring. Juksakai told them to go to the other shelter, and they gathered their things, avoiding her eyes. Maybe they could smell the creature on her.

When only Juksakai remained, Torak helped Renn out of her boots and gently rolled back her legging. She tried not to flinch, but the pain made her eyes water.

"But what *was* it?" said Juksakai again.

Torak didn't answer. He found his old Forest jerkin, and started cutting a strip for a bandage.

Renn said, "Eostra has the fire-opal. She's made tokoroths. I don't know what she's done to that owl, or to those dogs—if that's what they are—but she's made them her creatures. They seem to feel only the will to destroy."

Juksakai looked appalled.

Renn turned to Torak. "Those howls. Could you understand them?"

He shook his head. "It wasn't wolf talk, or any dog that I know. But it sounded as if there were several of them. Maybe a whole pack."

Renn stared into the fire. She could still hear those growls; that hungry, sawing breath. Eostra had reared a brood of killers. She had taken the Mountain for her own.

Shakily, Juksakai poured ice water into a rawhide bowl, added dried willow bark, and mashed it with a stub of antler. He set the bowl beside Renn.

"Let me," said Torak.

"I can manage," she muttered. From her medicine pouch she took slices of horsehoof mushroom and put them in the bowl. When the strips were soaked, she gritted her teeth and laid the freezing poultice on her ankle.

She could feel Torak watching her. They both knew what this meant. Five moons ago in the Deep Forest, she'd twisted her knee. It had been two days before she could walk without help.

Stupid, *stupid*! she berated herself. Out loud, she told Torak to pass the bandage, then bound her ankle firmly, without wincing, to show him it didn't hurt.

He wasn't fooled. "You won't be able to walk for days," he said quietly.

Juksakai nodded. "Tomorrow we'll carry her down to the sleds. She'll be all right with us."

"A day's rest here and I'll be fine," snapped Renn.

"No you won't," said Torak.

She glared at him.

Juksakai glanced from her to Torak, and muttered about rejoining the others.

"One day," said Renn after he'd gone. "Then we can head into the Gorge together."

Torak rubbed the scar on his forearm. "Juksakai tells me it's two daywalks to the Mountain. Souls' Night is only four days away."

"So there's time."

"No, Renn. Not for you."

"You can't decide that for me."

"I don't need to." He pulled on his boots. "I'll say good-bye now. I'm leaving at first light."

There was a ringing in her ears. This wasn't happening. "But—you can't go all by yourself."

"I won't. I'll have Wolf."

"He isn't here."

"He'll come."

"How do you know? You'll be alone. That's just what Eostra wants!"

He did not reply.

Something in his manner made her look at him, really look. What she saw in his face made her catch her breath. There would be no need to tell him of Saeunn's prophecy.

"You know," she said.

He nodded.

"How?"

"When I saw the Mountain." He touched his breastbone. "I felt it. Here."

Renn was silent for a moment. Then she said, "Prophecies can be wrong. We can prove it wrong."

"Not this time." He paused. "Many winters ago, on Souls' Night, my father woke the great fire and broke the power of the Soul-Eaters. I have to finish what he began."

"I know. But—"

"And maybe I can do it, even against Eostra. But the thing is, Renn—" He broke off. "The thing is, when I try to think about afterward—about going back to the Forest and being with you and Wolf and Fin-Kedinn—I can't see it. It's all just dark."

Renn stared at him, aghast.

She watched him roll up his sleeping-sack and gather his gear. "Where are you going?" she said.

"I'll sleep in the other shelter, head off at dawn. You stay here. Get some rest."

He wore his stubborn look, and she saw that it was hopeless. "As soon as I'm better," she said fiercely, "I'll catch up with you."

"No."

"I will. And I'll prove it. Here. Take my wrist-guard. That's a pledge." Somehow, she managed to untie the thongs and grab his wrist. She pushed back his sleeve and fastened the thin oblong of polished greenstone on his forearm. "There. You can give it back when I find you."

"You mustn't try to find me."

"You can't stop me."

"Renn, *listen*! That creature ignored me and went after you. Because Eostra wants me alive, at least until Souls' Night—but she doesn't care about you. Well, I do." He slung his bow over his shoulder. "Stay with the

Swan Clan. Get better. Go back to the Forest."

"No!"

"Good-bye, Renn. Whatever happens, you know—you must know how much I . . ." His throat worked. "May the guardian fly with you." Stooping, he kissed her mouth. Then he turned and ran out into the dark.

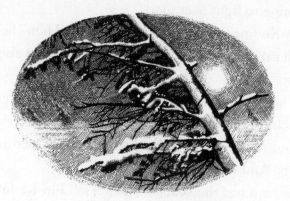

TWENTY-FOUR

The wind howled around the Mountains and swept across the fells. It stirred a thicket fringing a frozen lake, where men crouched around a fire.

A group of Rowan Clan had arrived on dog sleds, bringing three hunters from the Forest. They'd nearly missed Fin-Kedinn's camp, as he'd concealed it well, but in the end, their dogs had found him.

Etan of the Raven Clan spoke urgently to his leader. "Fin-Kedinn, we beg you, come back with us! Thull wouldn't have sent us if he wasn't desperate. The shadow sickness has spread throughout the clans. There aren't many people who are well enough to hunt. Those who are don't dare venture far, for fear of tokoroths. They're beginning to fight over food."

Fin-Kedinn took this in silence. Then he said, "Thull isn't the only leader among them. What about the others?"

"The Willow Clan Leader helped keep order for a while, and Durrain of the Red Deer. Then the sickness attacked them too. They've had to be confined to their shelters. And now Saeunn is dying."

"Saeunn has the shadow sickness?" Fin-Kedinn said sharply.

"No. She wore herself out tending her people. When we left, she was sinking fast. Thull says he can't lead without her. He's right. The clans won't listen to him alone."

"They'll have to," said Fin-Kedinn. "I must reach the Mountain."

"But *why*?" Uneasily, Etan peered into the thicket, where a shadowy figure hid beyond reach of the light.

"Who is that with you?" asked one of the Rowan hunters. "Why won't they come out and speak their name?"

Fin-Kedinn did not reply. The shadow in the thicket edged deeper into the dark.

"What do you hope to gain out here?" said Etan. "What can even Fin-Kedinn achieve against the evil one?"

"If we're to have a chance against Eostra," said the Raven Leader, speaking the name distinctly, "it won't be by might, but by Magecraft. I journey with one who knows these things; who knows how to find Eostra in the Mountain of Ghosts, and how to remain hidden from her and her creatures. That's all I can tell you."

Etan met his eyes. "Maybe this will change your mind. Saeunn herself sends word. She says only you can steady the clans."

"Saeunn was against my leaving," said Fin-Kedinn. "Of course she wants me back."

"She bids you remember what she saw in the embers. She says the spirit walker will die. Not even you can alter that. She says the place of the Raven Leader is with the living. She says you must return."

The fire sputtered. The hunters waited for Fin-Kedinn's answer. The figure in the thicket watched and listened.

Fin-Kedinn rose and strode to the edge of the trees, where a lone boulder stood guard over the lake. In the distance, the Mountains were black against the stars. They were still a long way off. If he returned to the Forest now, could he be sure that his companion would make the journey alone?

He stared at the sky. It gave him no answers. The World Spirit was far away, battling the Great Auroch. The troubles of men were not its concern.

And somewhere out there were Torak and Renn: isolated, vulnerable, like two tiny sparks about to be snuffed out by the night.

Fin-Kedinn ground his fist against the boulder. Duty called him to the Forest. His heart pulled him toward the Mountains.

The wind sank to a whisper. The granite was hard beneath his hand.

Fin-Kedinn turned from the darkness and walked back toward the fire.

TWENTY-FIVE

As Wolf slewed to a halt in the windy Dark, he sensed that his pack-brother was many lopes away. He'd made a mistake. He should never have run off into the Mountains.

He'd been gnawing the reindeer head near the great Den of the Taillesses when the eagle owl had swooped over him. He had known it was a trick, but he couldn't *not* follow. It had taken his cub.

Through Darks and Lights he had chased it, but now it was gone, and he didn't know where he was. His paws sank into the Bright Soft Cold, and the Mountains loomed over him. The wind carried the smell of ptarmigan and hare—but no Tall Tailless. Lifting his muzzle, Wolf uttered sharp, seeking barks. *Where are you?*

No beloved answering howl.

The wind veered and Wolf turned into it—and caught a smell he'd never smelled before. Dogs; but something was wrong with them. Wolf smelled that they were big and strong, cunning and full of hate. His claws tightened. Against such as these, Tall Tailless had no more chance than a newborn cub.

It was a blustery day, and the wind moaned through the Gorge of the Hidden People. Torak had heard no strange howls, but whenever a pebble fell, he started.

From time to time, he came across a boulder on which a spiral had been hammer-etched. Juksakai had said that his ancestors had made them to mark the trail to the Mountain; but no one had ventured in for many winters.

Who, then, had scraped the spirals clean of ice?

And where was Wolf?

Torak tried not to think of what Eostra's dogs could do to his pack-brother. And he couldn't even howl for him, except in his head.

In places, the snow lay thigh-deep; in others, Torak had to scramble over rocks scoured bare by the wind. He was soon sweating, but thanks to his Mountain clothes, he didn't get chilled. His jerkin had dense diverbird plumage at front and back, but looser-feathered ptarmigan under the arms to let out the sweat. His musk-ox wool socks were light as gossamer, yet incredibly warm. Pads of dried moss in his boots prevented blisters, and rawhide coils on the soles gave a good grip.

But nothing could protect him from the thinning air. His head ached. He felt constantly breathless. Worst of all was the knowledge that he was where he should not be.

The Gorge of the Hidden People was a bewildering maze of gullies and spurs and twisting valleys. Looming cliffs shut out the sky. The Redwater had fled underground. This was a world of stone.

And the Hidden People didn't want him here.

"They make you see things," Juksakai had said. "Once near the mouth of the Gorge, I found a snow-vole turned to stone. Another time I saw a great white bird vanish into the cliff."

"But what *are* the Hidden People?" Torak had asked. He knew they lived in lakes and streams and rocks; he'd even sensed them at times, and the memory was very bad. But he'd never paused to consider what they were, or where they came from.

"They used to be clans, like us," Juksakai had told him. "But long ago in the Great Hunger, they took to killing and eating people. The World Spirit punished them by decreeing that they must hide forever, only coming out when no one is near. That's why you never see them. If ever you get close, all you find are stones."

Torak sensed them peering at him from clefts in the rock face. He passed a ring of standing stones that leaned toward one another. Glancing back, he caught a blur of movement. As he walked, he heard a furtive rustling. It stopped when he did, but when he went on, it started again.

Around midafternoon, he paused for breath. "I mean you no harm," he told the dwellers in the rocks. "I seek the Soul-Eater. I have no quarrel with you."

A whirring overhead. He threw himself sideways. The boulder exploded on impact, pelting him with fragments.

Later, he heard the gurgle of water, and traced it to a spring in a gully. He found clumps of the heathery scrub Juksakai had used for waking fire; and an overhang that he could wall in with rocks, for a shelter.

No stones whistled down in the night, and he heard no strange howls. But there was no sign of Wolf, either.

Next morning the wind was gone. The stillness felt unnatural. Intentional.

Torak wasn't long out of the gully when he found tracks in the snow. Some time before, a pack of dogs had raced through the Gorge. Torak made out seven sets of prints, all bigger than any he'd ever seen.

Dry-mouthed, he drew his knife, and followed the trail around a spur.

The young hare had been torn apart. Dark-red entrails were flung across the snow like discarded rope. Ice-rimed eyes stared from its mangled skull.

Torak pictured the hare's desperate zigzag as the dogs ran it down. They had ripped it apart, spattering flesh and brains over thirty paces, but eating nothing. They had done it because they could.

Pity and disgust churned inside him as he muttered a prayer for the hare's souls. But as he headed off, it was for himself that he prayed. He had told Renn that Eostra wanted him alive. But alive, he reflected, did not necessarily mean whole.

The smell of sweat wafted from the neck of his robe. A dog would scent that from a daywalk away. *I'm frightened*, it said.

A thud behind him.

He spun around.

And sagged with relief.

Rek raised her head from the hare's skull and gave a preocuppied croak, then went back to pecking out an eye.

As Torak sheathed his knife, Wolf came bounding toward him over the snow.

Did you follow the owl? asked Torak when their first delirious greeting was over.

Yes, said Wolf. *But I didn't find the cub.*

I'm sorry.

Where is the pack-sister?

Safe, said Torak, *but she hurt her paw.*

You miss her.

Yes.

Me too.

Wolf snuffed the air. *Dogs. Far away.*

They're strong, and many, said Torak. *Much danger.*

Wolf leaned against him and wagged his tail.

They hadn't gone far when the Redwater reappeared, in an echoing channel under the cliffs. Rip and Rek flew to the top of a spur that cut across the Gorge, then back to Torak, calling impatiently. *Come on, it's easy!*

"No it's not," panted Torak as he and Wolf started to climb. The spur was made of knives. Some malign force had shivered its rocks into thousands of blades standing on edge. Even through his boots, Torak's feet were soon bruised. He hadn't gone far when he noticed that Wolf was limping. His pads were criss-crossed with cuts.

"I'm sorry," said Torak.

Wolf licked his ear.

In the Far North, Torak had seen sled dogs with paw-boots. The best he could do for Wolf was to bind his paws with strips of buckskin from his old jerkin. Wolf kept butting in to see what he was doing, and when the bindings were securely tied, Torak had to tell him sternly not to eat them.

He was so intent on watching Wolf that he didn't realize when they reached the top of the spur. Straightening up, he caught his breath. The Gorge of the Hidden People lay behind him. Above him loomed the Mountain of Ghosts.

Its summit pierced the clouds. Its glaring white flanks warded him back. *Sacred, sacred. A place of spirits, not of men.*

Sinking to his knees, he sprinkled earthblood as an offering. In hushed tones, he begged the Mountain to forgive him for trespassing.

Clouds closed in, hiding it from view. Torak didn't know if that was a good sign or bad.

To his right, a scree slope fell steeply to a shadowy valley. Ahead, glimpsed through the swirling whiteness, a huge boulder field led onto the Mountain. The Redwater cascaded from a small black cave mouth nestled in its midst.

Torak made out a spiral marker on one of the boulders. Filled with apprehension, he started toward it. Wolf padded after him, his tail down.

The boulders were treacherous with ice, and in places the snow was deep enough to make the going hard. They struggled past another marker, and another. They were now on the very Mountain itself.

And Torak had to find somewhere to camp.

They came to a spur where snow had drifted deep.

Torak was relieved. He preferred hacking out a snow hole to rearranging so much as a rock in this sacred place.

He didn't dare wake a fire. Huddled in his snow hole, he shared a scrap of smoked reindeer with Rip and Rek, while Wolf chewed the paw-boots—which, as his pads were already healing, Torak had given him for nightmeal.

As night deepened, Torak listened to the distant voice of the stream and the silence of the Mountain. It had allowed him to camp, but it could crush him in a heartbeat.

And Eostra . . . What of the Soul-Eater who waited within?

With the assurance of absolute power, she had let him venture through the Gorge; but she could send her pack to take him whenever she wanted. And the day after tomorrow was Souls' Night.

On his forearm, Torak felt the weight of Renn's wrist-guard. She had never seemed so far away.

He dreams it is summer, and he is playing with Wolf in a lake strewn with yellow water lilies. Wolf leaps clear of the water and lands with a splash. Torak dives, trailing silver bubbles of underwater laughter. Still laughing, he bursts into the sun. Everything feels *right*. His world-soul is a golden thread stretching out to all living things. And there is Fa, standing smiling in the shallows. "Look behind you, Torak!"

Torak jolted awake. He heard the boom of falling rocks. The ravens' stony alarm calls.

Yanking on his boots and grabbing his axe, he scrambled out of the snow hole—and into a wall of fog.

Rip and Rek were invisible; he couldn't see two paces ahead. He glimpsed Wolf, a gray blur racing over the stones.

Stumbling toward him, Torak saw that part of the spur had collapsed; a few boulders were still rolling to rest.

Wolf halted, his black lips peeled back in a snarl.

Torak followed his stare. In the fog, all he could make out were the rolling boulders.

Wolf's growls shook his whole body.

Torak narrowed his eyes.

Not boulders.

Dogs.

TWENTY-SIX

Relentless as a tide, Eostra's pack surged toward them through the fog.

They were bigger than any wolf or dog Torak had ever seen. He took in shaggy manes clotted with filth. Bloodshot eyes empty of feeling.

Slipping off his mittens, he tucked them in his sleeves. He gripped his axe. Beside him, Wolf wrinkled his muzzle and bared his fangs.

Torak uttered a deep grunt-growl. *Stay together.*

Wolf edged closer to him without taking his eyes off the pack.

Silently, the dogs came on, utterly concentrated on their prey.

Defiance surged in Torak. All right, then. Let's see you fight.

One huge black beast lunged at him.

He swung his axe. Wolf leaped. The creature drew back, melting into the fog.

Another tried, then two together: harrying, disappearing, but always spreading out to surround them.

Torak knew what they were doing. With wolves and dogs, most hunts begin like this. Make the prey fight, make it run. Find the weakest. Go after that.

The weakest was Torak. He knew it. Wolf knew it. The dogs knew it.

Grabbing a stone, he threw it as hard as he could, hitting a brindled monster on the shoulder. The dog twitched an ear, as if at an importunate wasp.

The ravens dropped out of the sky with furious caws, their talons skimming the marauders' backs. The pack ignored them. Cowed, Rip and Rek flew higher—as if, thought Torak, they were already circling a carcass.

He threw more stones, and the dogs withdrew into the swirling white. But he could feel the ring closing in.

His grip on his axe was slippery with sweat. An axe wouldn't be much use except in close combat, and if it came to that, he wouldn't stand a chance. The only weapon that would've been any good was his bow, and that was in the snow hole, five paces away. It might as well be five hundred.

With the speed of a striking snake, a huge gray beast went for Wolf. Wolf whirled, sank his teeth into its rump. With a yowl it ripped free and fled, spattering blood.

The pack went on circling.

Wolf shook himself, unhurt.

At the corner of his vision, Torak glimpsed a black blur leaping toward him. He swung his axe, struck a glancing blow on the skull. The creature fell with a thud, then sprang to its feet as if nothing had happened.

As the pack prowled around them, the brindled beast—the leader—walked stiffly forward and halted three paces from Torak. Torak felt Wolf tense for the attack. Urgently, he told him to stand his ground.

The leader's small, dull eyes fixed Torak's, and for an instant, he knew its mind. What it saw before it was not a boy, but a sack of meat, to be savaged till it moved no more. What kept that black heart beating was rage at all these running, howling sacks of *life*—this *life* which must be destroyed.

By an act of will, Torak tore his gaze away.

He had an image of himself lying dead. Then he realized that that was wrong, it wouldn't be *his* body; Eostra wanted him alive. This was about getting Wolf away from him: about slaughtering his pack-brother.

Two dogs sprang at him. Wolf darted to intercept in a flurry of fur and fangs. The brindled leader attacked Torak from behind. His axe caught it flat on the ribs. With a yowl it slunk back—but only a pace.

As Torak ran to help Wolf, the leader sprang again, seizing the hem of his tunic in its jaws, dragging him down. He lashed out. It dodged, hauling him after it, strong as a bear. Torak slipped, nearly lost his footing. He pretended to weaken, let the creature drag him closer— then brought down his boot, heel-stamping between the eyes. For a moment the great jaws loosened. Torak wrenched his tunic free and staggered back to Wolf.

With a wet slapping of jowls, the leader shook itself, then lowered its head for the next attack.

Three dogs sprang at Torak, four at Wolf. But in midair the marauders yelped and twisted, as if struck from behind. Stones came hurtling through the fog. The pack faltered, casting about for the unseen attacker.

Torak thought he glimpsed a pale figure vanish into the fog.

Who's that? he asked Wolf.

Tailless, Wolf told him.

More stones smacked into the dogs: now from one side, now from another. Confused, the pack turned from Torak and Wolf and sought its mysterious assailant.

Shakily, Torak touched his pack-brother's scruff. Wolf's rump was bleeding, his left ear torn, but his eyes were bright; he wasn't even panting.

Torak was. He couldn't get enough air into his lungs.

He thought fast. Whoever was distracting the dogs wouldn't be able to do so for long. They would be back. And although Wolf could keep up the defense all day, he, Torak, could not. Soon he would go down. And they would kill Wolf.

Behind him, Torak saw a narrow cleft on the other side of the spur: a crack in the Mountain. He backed toward it.

Wolf threw him a warning look. *No!*

Torak kept moving. Reluctantly, Wolf came too. The dogs, battling a hail of stones, didn't notice.

The snow was knee-deep, but at last Torak reached the end of the cleft. The relief when he felt solid rock against his shoulders! Now he *could* last all day: eating snow, warding off attacks which could come only from the front.

Abruptly, the hail of stones ceased. The invisible guardian was gone. For an instant, Torak wondered who it had been; then he forgot about that. Once again, the pack was moving in.

Beside him, Wolf bristled with dismay. He'd followed Torak out of loyalty, but this went against everything he knew: no wolf backs into a place from which there is only one way out.

And Torak couldn't explain why he'd done it, because

Wolf wasn't able to think like prey. Torak, though, found it all too easy; and he'd seen enough encounters between wolves and reindeer to know how it works. Wolves—and dogs—hunt those who run. If you're prey, your best chance is to stand and fight.

He was right, but he'd underestimated Wolf.

For an instant, the amber gaze grazed his. In that moment, Torak sensed what he meant to do. No, Wolf, no, it's just what they want! Too late. A gap opened in the pack—and Wolf shot through it. The dogs sped after him.

It all happened in the blink of an eye, but Torak knew that he must seize the chance Wolf had given him.

Jamming his axe into his belt, he reached for the rocks and began to climb.

The last thing he saw before he boosted himself up the cleft was Wolf racing down the slope with Eostra's pack on his tail.

TWENTY-SEVEN

Wolf flew over the rocks and the dogs flew after him. Wolf *hated* running away—but he had to save Tall Tailless.

Wolf was heading for a great slope of Bright Soft Cold. From the voice of the wind coming off it, he knew it was deep, maybe wolf high. So. The pack meant to chase him where even a wolf must flounder. But he *knew* this trick, he used it himself when he hunted deer. Did they think they could fool *him*?

Slowing his pace, he let the lead dog lope closer, till he caught the stony thud of its dark heart. It was snapping its chops, as if already tasting his flesh.

Too soon. As Wolf reached the edge of the Bright Soft Cold, he spun on one forepaw and leaped sideways onto solid rock. The dog behind him was too heavy, it couldn't turn in time. As Wolf sped off, he heard it thrashing and snarling in the Bright Soft Cold. Wolf threw up his tail. They might be bigger than him, but he was *faster*!

Although not by much. Already they were gaining on him again.

Over the pebbles he went, flicking his torn ear back to listen, the other ear forward for danger ahead.

He smelled darkness rushing toward him. The wind that blew from it made a booming sound—it was coming from underground. Suddenly there was no more stone in front and the Mountain opened to swallow him. Skittering to a halt, he saw that the crack was many paces across. From deep within came a howling cold.

In a snap, Wolf decided. Tensing his haunches, he sprang. His forepaws clawed the other side. Throwing his tail around and scrabbling with his hindpaws, he gave a tremendous heave. . . . He was up.

Baying in fury, the pack ran along the other side of the crack. Wolf lifted his muzzle in scorn. No dog—not even these—can jump as far as a wolf!

And yet—something was wrong. There weren't as many of them as before.

Where was the leader?

The lead dog stood at the bottom of the cleft and watched Torak climb. Its stare never wavered.

As his fingers sought the next handhold, Torak pictured Wolf racing over the snow with the pack at his heels. Wolf stumbled. A dog sank its fangs into his flank. They were on him, tearing him apart. . . .

Torak's axe-handle banged against his hip, wrenching him back.

They haven't got Wolf, he told himself. It's what Eostra *wants* you to believe.

The cleft was the height of four tall men, but narrow enough for him to climb by bracing one foot on either side. The fissured granite provided many hand- and footholds, and on a summer's day, Torak would have scrambled up it like a squirrel. But the rock was running wet and veined with black ice. His fingers were clumsy with cold. His mittens had come untucked from his sleeves and swung loose on their strings, but he dared not slip them on.

Pausing for breath, he craned his neck. The Mountain was lost in fog, but he glimpsed the top of the cleft. He was halfway there.

"Don't rush, Torak." In his head he seemed to hear the calm, steady voice of his kinsman Bale. The summer before last, the Seal Clan boy had taught him rock climbing. Bale had been patient, never imparting more than Torak could take in. "Try to keep your arms no higher than about shoulder height; that way, your weight will stay mostly on your feet. . . . And heels down, Torak. Standing on your toes only gives you leg-shake."

Torak's heels *were* down, but his legs were still shaking.

Below him, the brindled creature growled.

Torak glanced down.

Cold, cold, that stony gaze; waiting for this sack of meat to drop into its jaws. Its hunger sucked at his souls.

He screwed his eyes shut. Don't look, he told himself. Don't think about it. Put something else in its place. Think about Wolf and Renn and Fin-Kedinn.

The darkness in his head blew away like smoke dispersed by a cleansing wind.

Opening his eyes, Torak forced his numb fingers to seek another handhold.

He found his rhythm again, moving a hand, then a foot, then the other hand, the other foot. Smooth and fluid, like a dance. Nearly there.

The axe in his belt snagged on an outcrop and yanked him back.

He clung on with both hands, his right leg raised to find the next crack. But the next crack was too high— his foot couldn't reach it because the axe was wedged, holding him down.

Lowering his right leg, he tried to find the foothold he'd just relinquished. His boot brushed solid rock, he couldn't find it. Now his left leg, bearing his whole weight, began to shake. He couldn't keep this up much longer, he would have to reach down with one hand and free his axe. But then he would have only one hand and one foot on the rock; and that wasn't enough to hold him there. Again he seemed to hear Bale's voice. "If you remember nothing else, Torak, remember this. Always keep *three limbs* in contact with the rock. Move either an arm or a leg, but never both at the same time."

His left leg was trembling violently. No choice: he'd have to *pull* himself clear.

The knuckles of both hands whitened as he strove with all his might to haul himself free. The axe made a terrible grinding noise. His belt tightened about his waist as the axe-handle twisted downward. His arms shook with strain. With a jolt that nearly threw him off, the axe jerked free. He boosted himself up, and his free foot finally found the next crack.

Shuddering with relief, he braced both legs against either side of the cleft. When he'd stopped shaking, he made one last effort and hauled himself over the top.

Like a landed salmon he lay gasping, his cheek against icy stone. Before him stretched a plateau some fifty paces wide. It was shadowed by crags wreathed in fog, and littered with broken boulders which the Mountain had sent crashing down.

Torak got to his feet, and the freezing wind buffeted him, so cold it made his temples ache. He untangled his axe from his belt. It slipped from his hands and tumbled into the cleft. Aghast, he watched it clatter to the bottom.

The dog was nowhere to be seen.

Torak peered down, unable to take in the loss of his axe.

He felt eyes on him.

He turned.

Twenty paces away, on the rocks beneath the cliffs, stood the Eagle Owl Mage.

Her deathless, deathlike mask was the livid white of shattered bone. The slit of her mouth gaped in a soundless scream. One hand clutched a mace topped by a glowing red stone, the other a three-pronged spear for snaring souls.

Torak fumbled for his knife. He knew it would be useless against the Soul-Eater, but it had belonged to Fa, and it lent him the courage to stay standing.

The evil of the Eagle Owl Mage crackled like lightning, blasted him back.

He thought of Wolf, hunted by the pack. "Call them off," he panted.

The painted owl eyes glared. No sound issued from the slitted mouth.

"Call off your dogs from my pack-brother!" shouted Torak. "You've got what you want! Here I am!"

The Masked One never stirred, but behind her,

Torak saw shadows spread like wings. He felt her malice battering his mind.

Then from the nightmare mask came a cry that pierced his skull. Echoing from rock to rock, it grew; louder and louder, slivers of bone skewering his brain. . . .

Look behind you, Torak.

Torak glanced over his shoulder—and ducked too late. The eagle owl struck him on the side of the head. He staggered, swaying on the edge. Above him the owl veered for another attack.

At that moment, a great white bird came swooping out of the fog, its talons outstretched to strike the owl. The owl swerved to evade it, and flew around to come at Torak again.

He tottered backward and fell.

TWENTY-EIGHT

Torak woke up floating in a cloud. It was soft and light, and deliciously warm.

With an effort, he lifted his eyelids. Through a mist, he glimpsed white reindeer leaping over him. White wolverines ambled peacefully among white lemmings and willow grouse. A snowy musk ox grazed near a raven bright as frost.

"Am I dead?" he mumbled.

"I don't think so," said a voice that seemed to come from a great distance.

Torak sighed.

Later, it occurred to him that the voice had been right,

as he was still in his body. His outer clothes were gone, but he wore his jerkin and under-leggings. The cloud tickled his bare feet.

"Where am I?" he murmured.

"Here," the voice said quietly.

Torak tried to make sense of that. "Are you the Hidden People?"

A pause. "I hide. But I'm not one of them."

The mist began to clear. Torak smelled woodsmoke. He heard water dripping; the spitting of a fire. He felt the tightness in his chest that he only got when he was in a cave.

His eyes snapped open.

He was lying on a mat of hare-skins beneath a covering of musk-ox wool. The cave was so narrow he could have spanned it with his arms, but he guessed it must be deep. Beyond his feet, daylight rimmed a patchwork of hides that shut off the cave mouth. Nearer, a fire cast a ruddy glimmer. Torak saw piles of heather and dried musk-ox dung; and strings of herbs, mushrooms, and trout, hanging to smoke.

White reindeer and musk ox had been painted on the walls in gypsum. Lemmings, wolverines, and grouse, cramming every ledge, had been carved in slate and dusted with chalk. The white raven was real. It perched on a rock, peering at Torak. Feathers, legs, claws, even its beak were white. But its eyes were dark, and raven-keen.

Shakily, Torak sat up. He felt giddy and bruised, but he could move all his limbs, so he guessed that the snow and his bulky clothes had broken his fall. His head throbbed. The eagle owl had reopened his scalp wound, which someone had bandaged.

The eagle owl.

Everything returned in a rush.

"Who's there?" he said. "Where's my knife! Where's Wolf?"

No answer.

Torak staggered toward the cave mouth.

"Stop!" cried the voice.

Torak heard running feet and clattering claws. He pushed past the hides into an icy blast. Hands yanked him back from a dizzying drop. He sat down hard, and Wolf pounced on him, snuffle-licking his face and whimpering with joy. *You're awake! I hate these long sleeps! I'm here!*

Torak reached for Wolf's scruff. He stared up at the boy who had saved his life.

He appeared to be about Torak's own age. Grimy and thin, he was blinking and shielding his eyes from the light. He wore a shaggy robe of musk-ox wool, and had no visible clan-tattoos. But it wasn't any of these which made him extraordinary.

He looked as if someone had stolen all his color. His long, tangled hair was white as cobwebs. His brows and lashes had the hue of dead grass, his face the pallor of fresh-cut chalk. His pale-gray eyes made Torak think of a sky full of snow.

"Who are you?" said the boy with an odd blend of fear and longing.

"*What* are you?" cried Torak, struggling to his feet. "You took my clothes and my knife. Give them back!"

The boy stretched his lips in a gap-toothed smile that looked as if he hadn't used it in a while. "Your knife is safe." He pointed to a ledge. "You're dizzy. I made you sleep. You talked a lot."

"You're one of her creatures!" snarled Torak.

"Whose?"

"Eostra!"

"The one who has taken the Mountain?"

"Don't pretend you don't know!"

"Oh, I know. I've seen her." Torak saw the shadows under his eyes. This boy had endured days and nights of fear.

Or else he was a good liar.

"You must be helping her!" Torak insisted. "Why else would you be here?"

"I was here before. I—" He broke off, turning his head to listen. "I'm coming soon," he called.

"Who's there?" said Torak suspiciously.

"You should rest," urged the boy. "You're dizzy."

As he said it, the giddiness got worse. "Are you a

Mage?" Torak said. "Making me feel whatever you want?"

"A Mage? I don't think so."

Wolf was licking Torak's hand. Hazily, Torak saw that his pack-brother's wounds had been cleaned and smeared with salve, and that he seemed quite at ease with the stranger.

"At first he wouldn't let me near you," said the boy, holding out his fingers for Wolf to sniff.

"Why did you make me sleep?" said Torak, fighting to stay upright.

"I had to go and check my snares. I couldn't let you get away."

Torak blundered past him and grabbed his knife. "Give me my clothes. Let me out."

The cave was whirling. Gently, the boy took his knife and made him lie down on the hare-skins.

When Torak woke again, he was back under the musk-ox covering.

And he was bound hand and foot.

"Let me go."

"No."

"Why?"

"You'd get away."

"But I can't stay here!"

"Why?"

Torak gave up struggling and stared at his captor.

The boy's hare-skin boots had been clumsily patched with bits of lemming, and his robe had been made by someone who'd never learned to sew. He sat with his hands between his knees, gazing wistfully at Torak.

"Who *are* you?" said Torak.

The pale lashes flickered. "I'm Dark."

Torak snorted. "Why'd they call you that?"

"They didn't. They threw me out before I got a name, so I chose Dark. I thought it might help."

Torak felt a flicker of pity, which he swiftly suppressed. "If you have nothing to do with Eostra, how come she hasn't killed you?"

"I keep off her dogs and the child-demon things with my slingshot. That's how I helped you when the dogs attacked. And Ark guards me when I sleep."

"Who's Ark?"

On its perch, the white raven fluffed its head-feathers.

"If Eostra wanted you dead," said Torak, "she'd have found a way."

"Yes. I think she likes the power. For her, I'm a game." He gave Torak his odd, stretched smile. "But now I've got you. I'm not alone anymore."

Torak couldn't figure him out. He was scrawny, but he'd managed to get Torak into his cave, and he'd done a good job of tying him up. Wolf sniffed the bindings, but when Torak told him in a furtive grunt-whine to chew the ones at his wrists, Wolf simply licked his fingers.

"Are you hungry?" said Dark.

"No," lied Torak. "Who *are* you? How come you're here?"

Dark took half a dried trout from inside his robe and began to gnaw. "When my mother carried me in her belly, a white hare ran in front of her, so I was born like this." He touched his cobweb hair. "My mother said I was Swan Clan like her, but when I got older I began to see things, and they said I brought bad luck. My mother protected me, but when I was eight summers old, she died. Next day, Fa took me into the Gorge. I thought he was going to give me my clan-tattoos, but he left me. I kept the trail markers clear so he could find me again. But he never came back."

"Didn't you try to make your own way out?"

"Oh, no. I knew I had to stay."

Torak thought about that. "So you've been here ever since?"

Dark indicated the stone creatures thronging the ledges. "One for each moon."

"But—that must be seven winters. How did you survive?"

"It was hard," said Dark, picking a fish bone from between his teeth. "The first three winters, someone left food. After that, nothing. I was cold till I gathered the musk-ox wool. Once, my teeth went bad. They hurt till I knocked some out with a rock." He paused. "I was alone. Then I found Ark. Some crows were pecking her because she was white. I named her Ark—it was the first thing she said to me." He grinned. "She likes her name; she says it a lot!"

"So all this time, it's been just you and the raven?"

"And the ghosts."

Wolf got up and trotted deeper into the cave. Dark turned his head to listen.

"You—can see ghosts," said Torak.

Dark nodded calmly.

It was very still in the cave. Torak said, "Was that a ghost you were talking to before?"

"My sister, yes. But as she's a ghost, she doesn't remember she *is* my sister."

Torak peered into the shadows, but all he could see was Wolf, who sat sweeping the floor with his tail. He said, "Have you seen the ghost of a man who looks like me? Long dark hair? Wolf Clan tattoos?"

"No. Who's that?"

Torak did not reply. "But we are inside the Mountain? The Mountain of Ghosts?"

"Yes."

"Are there other caves?"

"Lots. I like the whispering cave, because of the ghosts. But I haven't gone there since she took it. She brought demons and the cold red stone."

Torak's heart began to pound. "How do you get there? To the whispering cave?"

"Many ways."

"Take me there."

"No."

"You've got to. How long have I been asleep?"

"Um—nearly two days."

"*Two days?*" shouted Torak. "But that means tonight is Souls' Night!"

His shouts brought Wolf racing to his side.

Now Torak understood why Eostra had let him escape: because he hadn't. It suited her to leave him cocooned like a fly in a spider's web, until such time as she had a use for him.

"Dark, listen to me," he said, forcing himself to keep calm. "Tonight the Soul-Eater will do something terrible. I don't know exactly what, but I know she means to conquer the dead, and use them to rule the living. You have to let me go!"

"But in your sleep you said she wants to kill you. You must stay with me. You're safe here."

"After tonight, nowhere will be safe, she'll be too strong! With the dead at her command, she'll rule the Mountains, the Forest, the Sea!"

"What's the Sea?" said Dark.

Torak let out a roar that shook the cave.

Wolf set back his ears and yowled.

Ark flapped her wings.

With a huge effort, Torak mastered his temper. "Maybe this will persuade you. In some way I don't understand, my father's spirit is tangled up with her. If I can stop her, maybe I'll help him, too. Now do you see why you *have* to let me go?"

A shadow crossed Dark's extraordinary face, and he seemed suddenly older. "My father left me. He never came back."

Torak set his teeth. "What if it was Ark who needed help? You'd do anything to save her, wouldn't you?"

Dark wrung his chalk-white hands till the knuckles cracked. Torak could see that he was torn. "Winters and winters I've been here," he said. "You're the first person, the first living person."

Sensing his turmoil, Ark flew onto his shoulder.

Wolf glanced anxiously from Torak to Dark and back again.

Torak waited.

Dark shook his head. "No. I can't let you go."

TWENTY-NINE

"*One day*," said Renn as she limped over the boulders. "That's all I asked. One day!"

A stone whizzed down and smashed behind her.

"Sorry," she muttered to the Hidden People.

They didn't like it when she spoke too loudly. They didn't much like her. But so far they'd tolerated her; maybe because of the little bundles of rowan twigs she'd left at every trail marker.

It had been two days since Torak left. The Swans had wanted to leave at once, but Renn had insisted that they remain at the mouth of the Gorge. She'd spent a desperate day in camp, grinding her teeth as she waited for her ankle to get better. Next morning she'd lied to the Swans that it was, and headed after Torak. They hadn't tried to stop her. They'd simply given her provisions and watched her go.

At first, things had gone well. Torak's trail had been easy to follow, and though her ankle ached, she could walk on it. She'd jumped at every sound, but her Mage's sense had told her that Eostra's creatures were far away. And in the afternoon, she'd made a heartening discovery: a rocky shelter that was unmistakeably Torak's. She'd spent the night in it, and fallen asleep planning what she would say when she caught up with him.

She'd woken stiff, cold, and scared. A pallid sliver of moon hung in the morning sky. Tomorrow night was Souls' Night.

She hadn't gone far when she found the bones of a hare, picked clean by ravens. Nothing odd about that; and yet her hand had crept to her clan-creature feathers. Malice hung in the air. Bad things had happened here. Evil had soaked into the rocks.

That had been a while ago, but she was still shaken. Her boots crunched noisily over frozen scrub and black lichen brittle as cinders. The glug of her waterskin sounded like footsteps. She stopped, to make sure that they weren't.

"They're not real," she said out loud. "There's nothing here."

The stones tensed. She felt the Hidden People watching.

Eostra was watching too.

Clouds began pouring over the edge of the cliffs. Stealthily, they swallowed the Gorge, folding Renn in a clammy embrace. Eostra hadn't sent her dogs to drive her back. She didn't need to.

Like a winged shadow at the corner of her vision, Renn felt the presence of the Eagle Owl Mage. Fog stole down her throat and took her breath. Her ankle throbbed. Her courage slunk away. Why go on, when she was doomed to fail?

She had an odd sensation of watching herself from above. There she was, a lame girl cowering in a ravine. She would never find Torak. He had left because he wanted to face Eostra alone: because he wanted to die, and be with his father. And soon that wish would be fulfilled.

In the distance, a raven croaked.

Renn raised her head. That was Rip.

Moments later, even farther off, she heard Rek answer him.

As Renn listened to their cries slowly fading, she clenched her fists. Rip and Rek didn't sound defeated.

They sounded intent on some mysterious raven matter of their own; probably concerning food.

As if in sympathy, her belly growled. Fog or no fog, she was hungry.

Opening her food pouch, she took out two strips of smoked reindeer tongue stuck together with marrowfat. Then she sat on a boulder and began to eat. It was the best thing she'd ever tasted.

She decided that her bow could do with some food, too. Juksakai had given her a bladder of oil from reindeer foot joints, which he'd said was better than anything for keeping wood and sinew supple, even in the coldest weather. Renn lavished some on her bow. Then she checked her arrows: a gift from Krukoslik, with fine quartz heads and white owl-feather fletching. "*Good* owls," she muttered under her breath.

The fog swirled about her angrily.

The food, the oil, the arrows: these had been prepared by kind people. The clothes they'd given her were meant to confer courage as well as warmth. The Mountain Hares had said that they always made the fronts of their robes from reindeer chest fur, "For in the breast of the antlered one, there beats a great heart."

A great heart. Renn's thoughts went to Fin-Kedinn. She sat straighter. "I'm bone kin to the Raven Leader," she told the fog—and it writhed at the resolution in her voice. "I'm Renn. I am a Mage."

As she headed off, the fog no longer seemed quite so thick.

Feeling more equal to the struggle than she had all day, Renn turned over what she knew of Eostra's plans.

The Eagle Owl Mage meant to live forever. She meant to eat Torak's world-soul and take his power.

Renn halted.

Until now, she'd never asked herself *how* Eostra meant to do that. But if she could work out how, then she might have some chance of stopping her.

The best Renn could come up with was a rite for *holding* souls which Saeunn had once told her about. This was carried out when a mother or father was grieving so fiercely for their dead child that they risked going mad. Their Mage would catch the newly disembodied spirit in a rowanbark box and tie it shut with a lock of the dead one's hair. The mourner must then live apart from the clan for six moons, with only the souls in the box for company. Then the souls were freed by opening the box and burning the hair on a hilltop, so that the smoke would waft up to the First Tree in the sky.

Taking off her mitten, Renn scratched her head. What did this have to do with Eostra?

Her fingers stilled.

Hair.

Your hair holds part of your Nanuak. That's why the Death Mark for the world-soul is daubed on the forehead.

And that, thought Renn in a flash of insight, is what the tokoroth was after on the night after the ice storm. Torak's hair. If Eostra could get some of his hair by Souls' Night, she could take his world-soul and his power.

It was horribly simple. And maybe it was also why Eostra had sent her tokoroth. She'd been taunting them, telling them that she could get Torak's hair whenever she wanted.

Renn began to run. She floundered through snowdrifts and slithered over icy scree. She ran past patches of bearberry, crimson as spilled blood.

A large bird swooped overhead, skimming her hood.

Its wingbeats faded. Renn hid behind a rock. The wingbeats were coming back. Too noisy for an owl, she thought.

Rip lit onto the rock and rattled an excited *kek-kek-kek!*

Renn gave an edgy laugh. Rip hitched himself into the air and flew off. *Quork!*

When Renn didn't follow, he flew back.

Renn chewed her lip. Torak's trail led straight ahead, but Rip wanted her to follow him down a gully.

Quork! he cawed impatiently.

Renn followed.

She hadn't gone far when the fog thinned, and she made out something lying on the rocks. Rip and Rek wheeled above it, as if circling a carcass.

Renn's belly turned over. It *was* a carcass.

Sound cut away as she stumbled toward it.

THIRTY

Darkfur's breath came in rasping coughs that made her flanks heave.

As Renn knelt beside her, the she-wolf raised her head and attempted one of her little greeting snaps. The effort was too much. She slumped back.

Drawing off her mitten, Renn laid her hand on Darkfur's side. She could feel each rib. The she-wolf hadn't eaten for days.

How had she managed to get all this way?

Renn pictured Darkfur hauling herself from the river after the owl's attack, and setting off: battered, longing for her cubs, determined to find her mate. Perhaps she'd been drawn by Wolf's howls; perhaps by the strength of the bond between them. With the resilience of wolves which surpasses that of the toughest man, she had survived the ice storm and made it across the fells. Renn remembered Krukoslik speaking of hunters finding a dead wolf, and leaving food for its spirit. Maybe that had been Darkfur. Maybe the kindness of strangers had saved her life.

Wrenching open her food pouch, Renn placed a slip of meat by the she-wolf's muzzle. Darkfur ignored it.

Rip flew down and sidled closer.

"No," scolded Renn. "She needs it more."

The raven gave her a reproachful look, and stalked off to sulk.

Renn nudged the meat closer. Still no response.

Puzzled, Renn touched one large black forepaw.

Darkfur tensed, and uttered a low growl.

Renn's alarm deepened. That pad was burning hot. Then she noticed that Darkfur's nose looked dull. Her tongue was tinged gray.

Renn leaned nearer—and recoiled at the stink. It wasn't hunger which had felled the she-wolf. The owl's claws had gashed her foreleg from shoulder to shin, and the wound was festering. Renn saw foul, oozing green pus.

Her thoughts raced. Darkfur lay in a hollow under a rock. It shouldn't take long to turn it into a shelter. Farther back in the gully, she'd passed a clump of the heathery plant which Juksakai used for waking fires. She had herbs in her medicine pouch—she'd refilled it before leaving the Swans—and she knew a healing charm.

It flashed through her mind that all this would lessen her chances of finding Torak, but she told herself the delay would be slight. Dress the wound, coax Darkfur to eat, then leave her to get better. How long could that take?

Sure of herself now, Renn worked fast. Soon the shelter was built and a small fire woken. At the foot of a boulder where a hawk had perched to eat its prey, she found the tiny skull of a snow-vole: strong medicine against fevers. Best of all, the purple droppings on the boulder led her to a nearby stand of juniper. That would be a powerful aid to the healing charm.

Back with Darkfur, she heated water and made a brew of crushed sorrel root, vole bones, and juniper berries. Cooling this with snow, she started cleaning the wound by trickling a few drops onto the injured shoulder.

Darkfur's growls shook her whole body.

Renn swallowed. She tried again. Same result.

She wished she was Torak, and could speak wolf. If only she could tell Darkfur that this would do her good. "Darkfur, *please*," she said. "I'm trying to help you."

Darkfur swiveled one ear.

"You have to let me clean your wound."

The green-amber gaze touched hers, then slid away.

Maybe that's it, thought Renn. Just talk.

"I'm—I'm sorry about the cubs," she stammered. "And that the owl hurt you. But Wolf is alive. You will see him again. Only you have to let me help you."

Darkfur remained tense, the sinews on her long legs standing out like cords. But she was listening.

Renn went on talking: softly, continuously. Praying that the she-wolf would hear from her voice that she meant no harm. The next time she dribbled medicine onto the wound, Darkfur lay quiet.

Washing the injured leg was agonizingly slow. Renn did as much as she dared, then prepared the poultice. She chewed juniper berries, then ground sorrel root with earthblood and juniper bast, and mashed the whole into a warm pulp.

Muttering the charm under her breath, she leaned closer, hiding the poultice behind her back.

Darfkur bared her fearsome white teeth.

Renn froze. Sweat broke out between her shoulder blades. When the she-wolf's muzzle relaxed, Renn slowly brought out the poultice.

Darkfur swung her head close to Renn's face. Renn felt her hot breath. She stared into the open jaws. "It—it's all right," she faltered. "Let me do this."

The jaws slackened. The she-wolf lay back and shut her eyes.

Trembling, Renn laid the poultice on the wound. Darkfur didn't stir.

The ravens edged in and made off with the meat. Renn was too drained to care. She heard them squabbling; then a sleepy rustle of feathers as they settled down to roost.

To roost?

She crawled out of the shelter.

While she'd been tending Darkfur, the rest of the day had slipped away. By now, Torak might already have reached the Mountain of Ghosts. Tomorrow night, when the sun went down, it would be Souls' Night.

Too late, Renn perceived Eostra's cunning. The Soul-Eater had allowed Darkfur to get this far for a reason: to keep Renn away from Torak. And it wasn't hard to work out why the dogs hadn't menaced them. They had other prey to hunt. Somewhere, in some lonely place, they were cornering Torak and Wolf. Renn saw their evil heads sunk between their shoulders as they closed in for the kill. . . .

Angrily, she pushed that away, and crawled back inside, where she found Darkfur twitching in her sleep.

Renn bit her lip. She knew she would have to spend the night here—but what then? Should she stay and look after Darkfur? Or let the she-wolf take her chances, and catch up with Torak?

Wolves heal much faster than people, but even so, the wound would need bathing and dressing. Perhaps another whole day would be lost.

Renn didn't know what to do. She felt pulled in

different directions by ropes of loyalty and love.

Beside her, Darkfur's tail thumped in her sleep. Her muzzle quivered. She was smiling. She gave an eager, keening whine. Renn's heart twisted with pity. In her dreams, Darkfur was calling her dead cubs.

Moments later, the she-wolf awoke. For an instant, her eyes glowed. Then the dream faded, and she gave a defeated sigh.

Gently, Renn stroked her forepaw. If she followed Torak and Darkfur died, how would she ever face Wolf? How would she face herself?

Her doubts fled. If she broke faith with Darkfur now, then whatever happened on the Mountain of Ghosts, Eostra would have won. The she-wolf had come through grief and hardship. Although Renn's spirit cried out to follow Torak, her mind was made up.

She would stay.

THIRTY-ONE

Torak had lapsed into furious silence. Dark was going through his things, asking questions. What's this green thing? A wrist-guard? Who made it? What's a foster father? Does he love you? Why is this pouch made of swans' feet? What's this horn for? Who made it? Your mother? Does she love you?

"Yes!" shouted Torak. Souls' Night was looming, and here he was, trussed like a ptarmigan, while this extraordinary boy examined his gear.

"There's a red hair around the top of the horn," observed Dark. "Is that your mother's?"

"No. It's a girl called Renn's. Don't touch."

Dark glanced at him. "Is she your mate?"

"No."

"But you like her."

"Of course."

"And she likes you."

"Yes!" he snapped.

Dark's pale face closed. His white eyelashes trembled. Suddenly he flung down the medicine horn and ran off into the shadows. Moments later he reappeared with Torak's clothes in his arms. "There." He threw them on the floor.

Ark croaked and flapped her wings. Wolf sniffed the hides. Torak watched Dark.

Brusquely, the boy drew his knife and cut Torak's bonds. "You're free. You can go."

Torak lost no time in getting dressed. As he was tying his belt, he said, "What changed your mind?"

Dark took a slate wolverine from a ledge and glowered at it. "All those people would miss you. Nobody misses me."

Torak paused. "I'm sorry."

Dark set down the carving. "I'll let you out."

The cave was deeper than Torak had thought. With Wolf padding behind him, he followed the glimmer of Dark's cobweb hair. The walls closed in. Snowy reindeer and musk oxen peered at him. Mindful of what else dwelled in the shadows, he said, "Your sister. Is she . . ."

"It's Souls' Night. She's gone with the others."

Torak felt icy air, and guessed that they'd reached the way out.

Dark jammed a slingshot into his belt and tied a bird-skin snow mask around his eyes. Torak cut the thongs on his mittens, so they wouldn't get in the way. Dark kicked aside a granite wedge and rolled away a boulder; but as he knelt to crawl out, Torak said, "Wait. I need you to do something."

The last time he'd worn Death Marks had been three winters ago, when he'd prepared to hunt the demon bear. Then, Renn had helped him. Now it was Dark who must daub the earthblood circles on his breastbone, heels, and brow.

As Dark stirred the ochre with thin fingers, he said, "I remember this. It's for dead people."

Torak didn't reply.

Dark's touch was light and skilled, and somehow reassuring. "There's some left," he said when he'd finished. "You must put it in your hair. There will be ghosts. You don't want them to come too close."

The red paste chilled Torak's scalp, but felt oddly comforting: maybe because his mother, who had been Red Deer, would also have worn ochre in her hair.

He rubbed the last of it between Wolf's ears. Soon his pack-brother would be alone on the Mountain. This might keep him safe.

The thought of leaving Wolf was unbearable; but so was the thought of taking him into the Whispering Cave and seeing him die.

With an irritable growl, Wolf wriggled free and shot out of the cave, followed by Ark and Dark. Torak crawled after them into the blistering cold.

He found himself on a precipitous, snow-covered slope. The fog was gone. The sky was an ominous yellow. Soon the Mountain would release its ghosts.

As his eyes became accustomed to the light, Torak realized that they were on its eastern face. The cleft he'd climbed lay somewhere to the west. Above him, the Mountain of Ghosts pierced the sky, its peak blazing in the last rays of the setting sun. The demon time was close.

Ark flew overhead, her white wings flashing. Wolf raced about, sniffing furiously, and stopping now and then to watch something move down the slope: something Torak couldn't see.

Dark sealed the entrance to his cave with a clever arrangement of rocks which hid it from view. "That's the way to the Cave," he said, pointing. "But it's steep, so first we have to head east, then loop back."

The hard-packed snow was treacherous, and Dark showed Torak how to kick into the snow with his toes. "You have to kick in *straight*, or your foot will slide out." A slab of snow broke off and exploded far below, demonstrating what would happen if Torak got it wrong. "Follow me," Dark called over his shoulder.

His voice rang out, and Torak was about to hush him when he thought, but what does it matter? Eostra knows we're here. This is what she wants.

The madness of what he was about to do struck him. He had no axe, no bow, and no plan, other than to find his way to the Whispering Cave and then—what? How did he imagine he could break the power of the Eagle Owl Mage? He would be as helpless as that young hare in the teeth of the pack.

Am I mad? he wondered. Is it because I've got too close to the sky?

Renn would have told him exactly what she thought with a roll of her dark eyes. Torak missed her so much, he felt sick.

"Here's where we turn," said Dark, waiting for him to catch up.

Wolf stood beside Dark, panting and swinging his tail. Sensing Torak's misery, he trotted back to him, his paws kicking up sparkling flakes of snow. *I am with you,* he told Torak.

"Not far now," said Dark.

They tramped on with the sun in their eyes. Glancing down, Torak saw that shadows were creeping up the Mountain. Soon it would be Souls' Night.

"There," Dark said quietly. "That's the way in. The Scar."

Shading his eyes, Torak saw a slash in the face of the Mountain. On either side, a hand had been hammer-etched in the stone. Lines of power emanated from the middle fingers, warding off evil.

In vain. Claw-marks had gouged the hands, annihilating their power so that Eostra might enter.

Torak felt the breath of the Scar chilling his face, stiffening the earthblood on his skin. Inside, death waited to claim him. Or worse: the unimaginable horror of being Lost.

Every shred of his spirit rebelled. I won't do it! Let someone else fight Eostra! It doesn't have to be me!

He fled, scrambling blindly up the slope. He tripped and fell to his knees.

When he raised his head, he saw that his flight had taken him much higher. He saw what until now had been hidden from view. The Mountain was indeed the easternmost peak, but what lay beyond it was not the edge of the world. Far below, marching away to the horizon, was another Forest.

In awe, Torak made out rowan and birch, oak and beech; pine and spruce standing guard over their slumbering sisters. And he, whose spirit had walked in the most ancient trees of the Forest of the west, now heard the call of the Forest of the east. *I am endless and enduring*, it murmured in his mind. *I give life to all who dwell in me. I am worth fighting for.*

Defiance kindled in Torak's souls. If he gave up now, then Eostra had won, and nowhere would be safe. The Soul-Eater would rip aside the skin between the living and the dead, and the balance of the world would be destroyed.

The sun sank. Brightness faded from the Forest. The demon time was come.

Torak trudged down the slope to where Wolf and Dark were waiting. He walked toward the Scar.

Two paces from it, he stopped. "Look after Wolf," he told Dark. "I've got to leave him behind."

Dark was horrified. "But—we're coming with you! You need me to show you the way."

"Dark, I don't think I'm going to live through this. No point you getting killed, too. As for finding the way . . ." He swallowed. "I think there are those inside who will lead me."

He knelt to say his last good-bye to Wolf. *Good-bye to Wolf.* It wasn't possible.

Don't think about Wolf left behind on the Mountain: bewildered, unable to grasp why his pack-brother has forsaken him.

Wolf snuffled his cheek, and Torak felt the tickle of his whiskers and the warmth of his breath. *Pack-brother*, said the golden eyes, as clear as sunlight in honey.

Wolf knew nothing of prophecies, or of Eostra's mad designs; but he would follow his pack-brother even into the terror of the Scar.

With a strangled sob, Torak buried his face in Wolf's scruff. Wolf whined softly and licked his neck. *I am with you.*

To leave Wolf behind would be a betrayal he would never understand; from which he would never recover.

"I can't," Torak said in a cracked voice. "Where I go, he goes."

As he rose to his feet, he caught a flicker of movement inside the Scar.

Wolf lowered his head and growled.

"Do you see it?" whispered Dark.

Deep within, on a shadowy pillar of stone, crouched a tokoroth.

Through a tangle of filthy hair, demon eyes glittered with malice. In silence the creature pointed one yellow claw at Torak, then swung its skeletal arm to the darkness within.

Torak glanced over his shoulder at the world he was about to leave. Then, with Wolf at his side, he entered the Scar.

"I'm coming with you!" cried Dark.

Unseen hands rolled a boulder across the entrance, shutting him out.

And the Mountain swallowed Torak and Wolf.

THIRTY-TWO

Renn fell to her knees before the sacred Mountain. Souls' Night. She felt the presence of the ghosts to whom it belonged.

With trembling hands, she made an offering of earthblood and meat. In a hushed murmur she begged the Mountain to let her pass. Then she shook what was left of the ochre over her hair, to protect her from the ghosts.

Above her the sky was a deep, twilit blue. The cold was savage. Her breath crackled in her nostrils. Her ankle ached, and her feet were bruised from the hill of vicious slate blades.

A few paces away, a shadow moved. It gave a low bark. Darkfur bounded toward her. Her tail was high, her fur fluffed up with excitement. Her starlit eyes glowed silver.

Renn's courage rallied. "Come on then," she said under her breath. "Let's check your paws."

To protect them from the hill of knives, Renn had cut up her food pouch and made paw-boots. They'd worked. The she-wolf's pads were barely scratched.

A good sleep and the poultice had done wonders for her, and after licking her wound clean and gulping most of Renn's supplies, she'd been a new wolf. By midday she had been circling the shelter, limping, but snuffing eagerly at the scent trail of her mate.

Renn, however, had been apprehensive after terrible dreams of ghosts who'd whispered with Torak's voice. And when she'd crawled from the shelter, the ravens were gone.

She and Darkfur had made good speed as they'd found their way up the Gorge of the Hidden People, the she-wolf trotting ahead, then doubling back for Renn. She didn't need to know wolf talk to interpret those impatient yips. *Hurry up! Can't you go any faster?*

At times, though, Darkfur would halt, and turn her head to watch something Renn couldn't see. Sometimes she wagged her tail. Sometimes her hackles rose.

A white bird flashed across the stars. Renn thought of

the white guardian in her vision, and rose to her feet.

To her right, a scree slope fell away sharply. Ahead, a boulder field led onto the sacred Mountain. The sky was immense and pitiless. No moon to give her courage. Only the cold stars and the red glare of the Great Auroch—and beyond, the endless dark.

Renn thought, perhaps Eostra has already won. Perhaps Torak is already a Lost One.

The stillness as she labored over the boulder field was terrible. The only sounds were the rasp of her breath and the creak of her clothes. Silent as a spirit, Darkfur raced ahead. A black wolf in blackness is hard to spot, and Renn had to follow the she-wolf's breath: little puffs of life in the desolation.

Suddenly, she saw Darkfur streak over a stretch of snow to a shadowy spur, where she raced about, sniffing excitedly. She vanished into a cleft. Renn heard echoing growls. Then she emerged and loped back to the spur, lashing her tail.

Renn hurried to investigate. As she drew closer, the hairs on her forearms rose. Someone had dug a snow hole. Around it was a mess of paw-marks. Huge. Not Wolf's.

Prickling with fear, she crawled into the shelter.

Her breath was loud in the cramped space. Her hands found a quiver of arrows. A food pouch. A waterskin. A sleeping-sack, rumpled and frozen stiff.

A bow.

Drawing off a mitten, she ran her fingers over the icy wood. There: the spiky Forest mark which Torak had notched in it last summer, matching the one his mother had carved on his medicine horn long ago.

Feeling sick, Renn set down the bow. The truth lay before her, crusted with frost. Some time before, Torak had scrambled from his shelter, leaving his gear behind. He had never returned.

Renn backed out and began to retch.

Darkfur gave a whine and shot to the edge of the scree slope, where she stood, listening intently.

Shakily, Renn straightened up.

Darkfur ignored her. Mewing, she ran in circles, as if she didn't know what to do. Then she leaped down the slope.

"Darkfur!" called Renn in a horrified whisper. "Come back!"

The clatter of pebbles died away. Darkfur was gone.

Renn's hand crept to her clan-creature feathers. She was alone on the Mountain of Ghosts.

Dimly, in the starlight, she made out the trail that led into the cleft, then out again; the swathe of churned snow heading east.

As she entered the cleft, she tripped over something. It was frozen to the ground: she had to wrench it free.

Torak's axe.

Renn knew at once what had happened. He had

climbed the cleft to escape Eostra's pack. He had fallen. The churned snow was the drag mark where someone had hauled away his body.

Renn dropped the axe and stood swaying in the gloom. "Torak!" The cry burst from her. "Torak! Torak!" The name echoed back and forth. *Torak! Torak!* Slowly it faded into the Mountain.

At the top of the cleft, a face peered at her.

Renn whipped out an arrow and nocked it to her bow.

"Don't shoot!" called a voice.

Renn tightened her draw arm and got ready to do just that.

Supple as a pine marten, a figure let itself over the edge and started climbing down.

Holding her aim, Renn took a step back.

With startling speed, the creature made its descent and leaped to the ground, spinning to face her. In one astonished heartbeat she took in a bone-pale face and a shock of white hair.

"Are you Renn?" panted the boy.

Her jaw dropped.

"Quick!" He grabbed her wrist. "We've got to save Torak!"

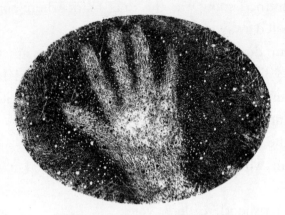

THIRTY-THREE

Flames leaped. Shadows reared. On its pillar, the tokoroth clutched a sputtering torch and glared at Torak.

He glimpsed glistening fangs and hair heaving with lice. He saw unblinking eyes ringed with chalk to give them the stare of an owl. Then the creature sprang away, plunging him in darkness.

Slipping off his mittens, he drew his knife and followed.

The tunnel was cold; he felt his way through a dank cloud of breath. Shadows scuttled. His hand moved over rock as ridged and slimy as guts. In a crack, something scaly withdrew from his touch.

Around him he felt the awesome weight of the Mountain. He was inside it: this vast, ancient creature which had only to twitch, to crush him to pulp.

Behind him came the subdued click of Wolf's claws. He'd stopped growling, and hadn't tried to attack the tokoroth, perhaps sensing it would stay out of reach. But what alarmed Torak was that the tokoroth ignored Wolf, as if it knew that he posed no threat.

As they went deeper, Torak began to regret having let his pack-brother come with him. Eostra would never allow Wolf to reach the Whispering Cave. She would find some way to separate them—and Wolf would be killed.

He wondered how many more tokoroths lay in wait. Where was Eostra's pack? Her owl?

Crouching, he asked Wolf if this cub-demon was the only one.

More, replied Wolf, his whiskers brushing Torak's eyelids. *Can't smell where.*

Up ahead, the tokoroth bared its fangs and snarled at them to keep up.

On they went, always downward. The cold lessened. Torak felt an uprush of warmer air. Strange signs loomed at him from the dark. A chalk zigzag. A yellow handprint. An alarming charcoal creature with many limbs. Were they a warning? Or had they been put here to keep the demons behind the rocks?

His groping fingers found a nest of pebbles, smooth and rounded as eyes. A memory surfaced from three summers ago: the riddle of the Nanuak. *Deepest of all, the drowned sight.*

Behind him, Wolf gave a low *uff!*

The tokoroth disappeared around a corner.

Torak felt his way past—and jolted to a halt.

Firelight glimmered beyond an arch of white rock; around it, a chaos of red handprints: *Go back, go back!*

Then everything happened at once. Torak saw the tokoroth douse the torch in a pool and scramble up the arch. Something came crashing down behind him: a wall of rawhide, barring his way. On the other side, Wolf was yowling and scrabbling to reach him. Torak tried to cut through, but the rawhide was tough—his knife bounced off. The tokoroth dropped on him like a spider, gouging at his face. As he sank to his knees, it yanked back his hood to throttle him. He slashed with his knife. The tokoroth shrieked, let go of his hood. Torak grabbed its arm and twisted. It squirmed out of his grip and vanished through the arch.

Panting, sick with the demon stench, Torak hauled himself upright. He stumbled, took a step back.

Into nothingness.

Wolf lunged and snapped at the cub-demons, and they fought back with their great stone claws.

Wolf pretended to spring one way, they leaped after him; he turned the other way, sinking his teeth into a scaly leg. The cub-demon howled and dropped its stone claw. Another bit Wolf's shoulder. He went for it, missing by a whisker. Both demons fled up the rocks where he couldn't reach.

It was too dark to see, but he sensed them. He heard their breath; the lice crawling on their flesh. Why didn't they attack?

In a snap, he knew. They might be demons, but they were in tailless bodies, so they had only feeble tailless ears and noses. If Wolf didn't move, they didn't know where he was.

Quietly, he closed his muzzle and took a silent sniff.

The stink of blood and hate was all around; but it was strongest above.

He heard Tall Tailless yowl on the other side of the hide. Wolf couldn't bear it, he leaped at the hide—and the cub-demons were on him.

They were quick, but Wolf was quicker. Whipping around, he sank his fangs into a bony neck. It snapped. The demon went limp. Wolf smelled the other and gave chase. It disappeared over the hide.

Wolf went to sniff the fallen tailless cub to make sure it was really Not-Breath. Yes. The meat was cooling. But Wolf saw the demon which had hidden inside the carcass slip out and scurry off to find a new body. He raced after it, cornered it in a Den where it couldn't escape, and chased it into the rocks. There. Now it couldn't get out again.

When he got back to the hide, he found the Breath-that-Walks of the tailless cub shivering beside its carcass. It was bewildered. After so long trapped with the demon, it didn't know what to do.

Wolf felt a lick of pity. It was only a cub. He nosed it up the tunnel toward the others. Go on, up there. You won't be lonely, we passed lots of your kind on the way down.

Whimpering, the Breath-that-Walks wandered off to find its pack.

From the other side of the hide came many noises. Wolf caught the growls of dogs and the click of cub-demon claws; the sly hiss of owl wings; and the distant whisper of a Fast Wet, all coming from far below.

He smelled his pack-brother, and another tailless he'd once known, but couldn't remember. Then the air shifted and he caught a smell that made his fur stand on end: the Stone-Faced One with the terrible, stiff muzzle.

Wild to reach his pack-brother, Wolf made a desperate leap at the hide. It was too high, he couldn't get over. He tried to tear it with his fangs, but it was too flat, he couldn't get his jaws around it. He had to find another way.

Turning tail, he hurtled up the Den. Through the

twisting tunnels he loped, bumping his nose and stubbing his paws. He burst into a bigger Den, where air from many smaller ones swirled around him.

Faint and far, he caught a scent that gave him hope. It was the scent of the new tailless with the white head-fur, and with him—Wolf could hardly believe his nose—*with him was the pack-sister.*

THIRTY-FOUR

"Who *are* you?" demanded Renn.

"Dark," the boy replied.

"*What?*" Twisting out of his grip, she drew her knife.

"My name. It's Dark!"

Renn tossed her head. "Whoever you are, you say you know Torak, but how do I know that's true?"

"I knew your name, didn't I?"

"You could've made him tell."

"You've got red hair. He's got a strand of it around his medicine horn. There! Now d'you believe me?"

Renn hesitated. "Where is he?"

"I *told* you, in the Mountain! I tried to go in too but

they shut me out. But there's another way in. You coming or not?"

Still she hung back.

A white bird swooped onto his shoulder.

A raven. A white guardian.

Renn threw off her waterskin and sleeping-sack. "Let's go," she said.

Grabbing her wrist again, he set off at a run, the white raven flying ahead. The boy called Dark must have the eyes of a bat to see in this murk—Renn could hardly make out the ground in front of her—and he was sure-footed. "I won't let you fall," he told her, as if he'd heard her thoughts. And somehow, she believed him.

After a stiff, winding climb her ankle was hurting, and she was relieved when he halted at the foot of a rock face.

At least, she thought it was a rock face. Clouds blotted out the stars; the night was black as basalt. She watched the raven fly off, a white glimmer swallowed by the dark.

"Light," muttered the boy, dropping to his knees. A birch-bark torch flickered awake, lighting his strange, pale face. "In there," he said.

Renn's belly clenched. It was a jagged fissure, like a mouth with broken teeth, and hardly big enough for a badger. They would have to crawl in on their bellies.

"I can't go in there," she said.

"You won't get stuck. I'll go first, you push your axe and bow in front, I'll take them. It'll be all right, you'll see."

As Renn crawled in after him, she felt the stone jaws clamp shut, squeezing the breath from her chest. She wriggled forward, trying not to think of the Mountain on top of her. Panic surged. Her arms were squashed against her chest. She couldn't move. She was stuck, as she'd been stuck in the Far North. But this time she wasn't getting out.

"We're through," said the boy, grasping her hood and hauling her into an echoing space.

She bumped her head, and gave a jittery laugh.

"Hush! Some of these stones are loose, you could start a rockfall. And watch out for holes."

It was frightening, seeing only a pace ahead. Beyond the jolting torchlight, the dark was so intense that it pressed on her eyeballs.

With an arrow she probed the ground ahead. She tripped. Her groping hand found something smooth and domed. A skull. Her whimper brought the boy running back. The light revealed the skull of a bear: huge, drowned in stone.

"Yes, lots of bones," said Dark. "From the old times, when the Mountain was more awake. It drowned many creatures."

As they went deeper, Renn heard water trickling.

She felt cold air from unseen tunnels. She glimpsed wet gray pillars clustered together. As she passed, shadows darted. She averted her eyes from the Hidden People of the Mountain.

"Careful, that's deep," warned the boy.

She stepped over a crevice, and caught a whisper of water far below.

Dark stopped so abruptly that she walked into him.

"What is it?" she said.

"It's shut," he said blankly.

A boulder blocked the tunnel. On it, an image had been daubed in gypsum, so that it glowed sickly white. An enormous owl. Its body was turned away—Renn saw its wings folded over its back—but its head was twisted around to glare at them. The meaning was plain. *Eostra sees all.*

"She knows we're here," said Renn.

"Of course she knows," said Dark.

He moved aside, taking the light with him, and the owl sank into shadow. Renn still felt its glare.

"I think there's another tunnel," murmured Dark, trailing his long pale fingers over the rocks, as if feeling their message. "Ah. That's it!"

He led her over a rock pile, then down into a clammy hole. This tunnel was narrower—they squeezed sideways—but to Renn's relief, it soon opened out.

Again Dark halted. "I don't remember this."

Raising the torch, he showed Renn a cavern roofed with folds of yellowish rock. Three tunnels yawned. The left one was low, fringed with dripping stone teeth. The middle one opened above a reddish stump like a severed limb. The third was the biggest, cut in two by a spear of stone jutting from the floor.

"Which one?" said Renn.

"I don't know. They all feel wrong. I think—"

"*You don't know?*" Pushing past him, Renn ran to the first tunnel and placed her hands on the edge, avoiding the stone teeth. The rock throbbed beneath her palms with the unclean heat of the Otherworld.

She ran to the tunnel with the stone spear. She felt the same pulsing demon heat.

Desperate, she scrambled up the stump and groped for the third opening. For a moment, the rock seemed to buckle under her fingers as demons jaws gaped to bite.

She pulled back. "All three have demons behind them."

"That's what I was going to tell you," said Dark.

"So which one do we take?"

"Don't move," he said in an altered voice.

"What?"

"Sh!" He jerked the torch upward.

In a crack above her head, Renn made out another stone owl. Its eyes were shut, its tufted ears erect.

"Climb down as quietly as you can," said Dark.

The owl opened its eyes and hissed at her.

With a cry Renn fell, knocking Dark backward. The torch went flying. Just before the blackness came down, Renn saw the eagle owl spread its wings and glide away.

Silence. A distant splash.

"That's the torch," said Dark.

"Have you got another?"

"No."

Panting, Renn got to her feet. "What do we do now?"

"I don't know."

Renn jammed her knuckles in her mouth. Somewhere in this terrible Mountain, Torak was facing Eostra alone.

A cold hand touched her wrist.

"Is that you?" she whispered.

"What?" said Dark, some paces away.

A chill finger touched her cheek.

"Stop it!" she cried.

"I didn't do anything!"

Renn screwed her eyes shut. She opened them. She saw. It wasn't possible in this darkness, and yet—she *saw*. "Do you see it too?" she breathed.

"I see it," Dark said softly. "But I don't know who it is."

Renn did. It was indistinct, as if in a mist, yet it seemed to hold its own light, as spirits do. Renn's fear drained away, leaving only a distant sense of loss.

Before her stood the wizened figure against whom she had rebelled all her life. For the last time she took in the flinty gaze; the lipless mouth which had never been known to smile.

Noiselessly, it extended one frail arm and pointed at the tunnel of the stone spear.

"Thank you," murmured Renn. "Thank you . . . And may the guardian fly with you." With both hands on her clan-creature feathers, she bowed to the spirit of the Raven Mage.

When she straightened up, it was gone.

Renn hoisted her quiver and bow higher on her shoulder. Then she reached out and took Dark's hand. "Come," she told him. "We know the way now."

THIRTY-FIVE

Torak was tumbling down a waterfall of stone. The ground rushed to meet him. Pain exploded in his shoulder and skull.

He lay still. His cheekbone hurt savagely, but he could move his arms and legs. Somehow, he'd kept hold of his knife.

Above him the stone waterfall disappeared into the dark. Unclimbable. No getting back. He thought, at least Wolf isn't here. At least he's got a chance of getting out.

He had a sense of a vast, shadowy cavern. Stone had once flowed like honey: dripping, pooling, then freezing hard. Twisted fangs of rock hung down; others jutted from the floor to meet them. Like teeth, thought Torak. *Oldest of all, the stone bite.* I'm in the jaws of the Mountain.

Firelight glimmered. He caught the whisper of water far below. Closer, he heard the rhythmic clink of bones. A voice chanted.

By power of bone
By power of stone
By power of demon eye
Eostra summons the Unquiet Dead
Eostra binds them to her!

Torak stumbled toward the light. No point trying to hide. She knew he was there.

Then he saw it.

In some ancient catastrophe, rocks had fallen in a pile as tall as two tall men. On the pile rested a slab of black stone, where a fire burned. Behind this altar, flanked by a pair of tokoroths rattling bones, stood the Eagle Owl Mage.

Her feathered robe seemed to gather the darkness to it, but her mask glowed ghastly white. In one corpse hand she grasped the mace which bore the fire-opal; in the other, the three-pronged spear for snaring souls.

By power of bone
By power of stone
By power of demon eye . . .

Torak tried to speak, but his mouth was too dry.

The arms of the Masked One rose, and her winged shadow engulfed the cavern. The tokoroths groveled, their evil child-faces alight with terror and adoration.

"You know I'm here," panted Torak. "You know I'll stop you."

The Masked One never faltered in her chant, but her spear swung around and pointed at him. At the foot of the rock pile, seven pairs of eyes lit up. Dark shapes sped toward him.

Jamming his knife into its sheath, Torak kicked off his boots and scrambled up the nearest fang of rock. The pack was almost upon him. Heaving himself onto a ledge a few fingers wide, he drew up his legs. The dogs swarmed about his refuge, leaping, snapping. Their breath scorched his bare feet, their jaws clashed empty air. Snarling, they fell back and sprang again, their hatred sucking at his souls.

An arm's length above him, his rock fused unevenly with a hanging tooth. He could climb higher. But then, a tokoroth could climb down. A shadow swept toward him. He lashed out with his knife. The eagle owl veered and flew back to its mistress.

Streaming sweat, Torak clung on. The fire's bitter smoke was making his head spin. Through it he saw the Soul-Eater set aside her spear and begin to wind a cord around the fire-opal. A sigh broke from the tokoroths.

With frenzied lust they rattled their bones.

Firelight struck glints of russet and gold in Eostra's cord, which was braided, like hair. As Torak watched her wind it about the stone, he felt himself drawn deep into the heart of the fire-opal.

It was the terrible scarlet of a lethal wound. It was beauty and suffering and mad desire. It was the glare of the Great Auroch in the winter sky, and it blazed with all the pain it had ever created.

Suddenly, the Soul-Eater ceased her chant. In a grating whisper, she uttered, one by one, the names of the Unquiet Dead.

The shock was so great that Torak nearly fell. At last he understood what she meant to do. And he couldn't stop her. He could only huddle on his perch like a pigeon about to be snatched by a hawk.

His medicine pouch dug into his hip. The horn was empty, it couldn't help him now.

And yet.

At the cost of her life, his mother had made a pact with the World Spirit. The World Spirit had made him the spirit walker. He owed it to her to use his gift one final time.

Dashing the sweat from his eyes, he called to the Soul-Eater. "You think you've got me! You think I can't reach you! You're wrong!" His voice sounded reedy and frightened.

Climbing to where the upward and downward fangs fused, Torak straddled the join. Now, though his legs hung down, the pack couldn't reach. Swiftly, he lashed himself to the stone with his belt. Then he took Saeunn's black root from his pouch and crammed it in his mouth.

Pain clawed his innards. He cried out . . .

. . . and his voice was the rasp of the Soul-Eater, summoning the Unquiet Dead.

Through her eyes and her slitted mask, Torak peered at the senseless body of the spirit walker. His flesh was gray; and gray the flames that leaped on the altar. All was gray, save the cold red heart of the fire-opal.

Deep in her freezing marrow, Torak's spirit strove to make her grasp a rock and shatter it, but her will was the strongest he'd ever known. Her will turned his to stone. This was her strength: that she felt no pleasure, no pain, *nothing* save the hunger for eternal life. Her tokoroths were not tortured children possessed by demons, but creatures created to do her will. Her dogs were merely weapons to be used and flung aside like broken flints. The boy on the rock was the husk of the power she craved; tear away that husk and the power became hers. *This* was evil and it was cold, cold. Torak's spirit drowned in it.

Abruptly, Eostra's voice ceased. The tokoroths' rattles stilled.

In the silence, the Masked One cast a rawhide

shield across the fire, and its light was quenched. In the darkness, she spoke.

Sleek as the seal . . . the cunning one,
Tenris . . . Come forth!

Almost imperceptibly, the cavern filled with the lapping of waves. Behind the altar, smoke thickened—coalesced—and formed the figure of a man. Through the eyes of the Soul-Eater, Torak perceived a handsome, ruined face; he heard a voice as smooth and strong as the Sea.

Tenris is come.

Chanting, the Masked One raised the rawhide from the altar. Smoke billowed, flames leaped. She quenched them again.

Mighty as oak, the strongest one,
Thiazzi . . . Come forth!

A rustling of leaves. A hulking shadow loomed.

Thiazzi is come.

Again Eostra chanted. Again she quenched and revived the fire.

Swift as the bat, the twisted one,
Nef . . . Come forth!

The leathery rustle of bat wings. Swirling motes came together and made the limping one.

Nef is come.

Cowering in Eostra's marrow, Torak could only witness her summoning the Unquiet Dead; and they were hers to command, bound by the power of the fire-opal.

In the darkness of her mind, Torak saw her vision of what was to be. *On Mountain and Ice, in Forest and Lake and Sea, the clans cower in dread before Eostra, who rules the living and the dead . . . Eostra, who lives forever.*

Eostra was invincible. Everything Torak had fought for over three long winters had been for nothing.

The Soul-Eaters were back.

THIRTY-SIX

Deep in the Mountain, Wolf heard the rustling of leaves.

Leaves?

He slewed to a halt. That didn't fit.

Was this another trick of the Hidden Ones? They hated him being here, they hated *anyone* in the Mountain, they kept scattering sounds and smells, so that he couldn't tell where they were coming from.

Wolf raced on, though he didn't know where he was going. He'd been running forever through this terrible, winding Den. He'd lost the scent of the pack-sister; all he could smell was wet rock and frightened Wolf. He was thirsty, his flanks hurt from the cub-demons' claws, and he *still* couldn't find Tall Tailless.

He reached a place where the Den widened and the breath of the Mountain ruffled his fur. He found some Wet in a dip and snapped it up, ignoring the stone bones lying nearby. They were just another trick; he'd tried one before, and nearly broken a fang.

Suddenly, he jerked up his head. A faint scent brushed his nose. Trembling with eagerness, he took deep sniffs to make sure. *Yes!* His pack-brother!

The scent was trickling from above. Rising on his hind legs, Wolf placed his forepaws on the rock. Too dark to see, but he felt the breath of a tiny Den. He leaped— scrabbled—he was in.

The Den was so small he had to flatten his ears and crawl on his belly. It scraped his sides and squeezed till he couldn't breathe. Then it spat him out and he fell, bashing his nose on a rock.

A torrent of smells whirled around him. The demon stink; the Not-Breath smell of the Stone-Faced One; the rich scent of the tailless whom Wolf now remembered from long ago. *And the scent of his pack-brother.*

Wolf flew through the dark. The tunnel was narrow and twisty as guts, but he caught the snarls of the pack. They had a hollow sound which told Wolf he was heading for a very big Den indeed.

He heard the familiar whine of the pack-sister's

Long-Claw-that-Flies, and the swish of owl wings. He quickened his pace. Hunting demons was what he was for.

The mouth of the tunnel was drawing nearer, and Renn quickened her pace.

"Not so fast!" warned Dark.

She ignored him. She could hear the clink of bones and the death-rattle chant of the Soul-Eater.

By power of bone
By power of stone
By power of demon eye
Eostra summons the Unquiet Dead
Eostra binds them to her!

Renn tried to remember a severing charm to counter the spell, but Eostra's icy will froze her thoughts. *None can hinder the Masked One.*

Renn reached the mouth of the tunnel.

Dark yanked her back.

The tunnel opened dizzyingly high, near the roof of the cave. There was no way down.

Biting back a cry, Renn sank to her knees and peered over the edge. Through a thicket of huge stone teeth, she saw that the cave was split by a chasm that zigzagged across it like black lightning. On the near side, a fire burned on an altar wreathed in smoke. Below this, shadows prowled at the base of a pillar whose top she couldn't see. Even from far away, she felt their hatred, and knew that this was Eostra's pack. There was no sign of Torak.

Eostra summons the Unquiet Dead . . .

Renn flung down her weapons. Her axe and bow were unhurt, but her quiver had been squashed when she'd squeezed through a gap, and only three arrows remained intact.

Eostra binds them to her!

The smoke parted, and Renn caught a fleeting glimpse of the Masked One. She saw a livid hand pass over the mace that held the fire-opal. She saw its scarlet light bleeding through a shadowy network of cords criss-crossing the crimson stone. She grabbed an arrow. Eostra sensed the threat and cloaked herself in smoke.

"Can you feel them?" whispered Dark, kneeling beside her.

"Feel what?"

"Down there in the smoke. Something terrible."

"I can't see anything."

"Neither can I. But I feel them."

Renn felt them too. There was more in the Whispering Cave than Eostra and her minions.

"It's the smoke," she breathed. "It's part of the spell. Don't look."

But Dark couldn't tear his eyes away. Neither could she.

The Soul-Eater broke off her chant. Blackness descended on the cave. In the silence, she spoke.

> *Subtle as snake, the seducer . . .*
> *Seshru . . . Come forth!*

Renn's flesh crawled.

The cave seemed to fill with a thin, echoing *hissss*.

This can't be, Renn told herself. It cannot be.

As she watched, the smoke swirled to form a sinuous shape. . . .

No. Seshru is dead. Your mother is dead. You put the Death Marks on her. You watched them lay her body to rest.

The chanting resumed. After an endless time, it broke off again. Once more, the fire dimmed.

> *. . . Narrander . . . Come forth!*

From the far side of the cavern, a man's voice rang out. "Narrander comes."

Renn caught her breath. She knew that voice.

"Your spell is flawed," it declared. "It holds the hair of a living man."

No answer from Eostra.

"Who *is* he?" said Dark.

Renn didn't reply. The past was coming together like pack ice as she watched the man emerge from the shadows.

The eagle owl swooped toward him. He warded it off with his axe. His gait was unsteady. Tattered hides flapped about his scrawny limbs. Renn knew that if she were closer, she would see a tangled beard glistening with slime. A filthy, one-eyed face as rough as bark.

The seventh Soul-Eater. He had hinted as much at their first encounter. *Before the flint bit him, he was a wise man. . . .*

"Narrander died," rasped Eostra from the smoke. "He died in the great fire."

"Another died!" bellowed the Walker. "He should have *lived*! The Walker ends it now!"

"None can hinder the Masked One."

The Walker roared and threw himself at the rock pile—but before he could reach it, he lurched to a halt. The chasm was too wide. He couldn't get across. "He should have *lived*!" His howl filled the cave with pain.

Suddenly, Renn saw the small, hunched figures clinging to the rocks above his head. Desperately, she took aim. Dark loaded his slingshot.

They lowered their weapons. The tokoroths were way out of range.

"Above you!" shouted Renn and Dark together.

The Walker glanced up as the first rock struck. He sank to his knees. Another rock hit. He fell to the ground at the edge of the chasm. His axe dropped from his hand, and a moment later there came a distant splash. The Walker lay without moving. Renn had never hated Eostra as much as she did then.

"I see Torak!" hissed Dark. Pulling her sideways, he pointed—and at last she saw him.

Torak was halfway up the pillar around which the pack prowled. He was tied by the waist, his head sunk on his chest. He wasn't moving.

"Torak!" screamed Renn.

No response.

He must be either stunned or spirit walking. She refused to believe that he was dead. Clenching her jaw, she got ready to shoot. How many dogs? Six? Seven? And only three arrows.

A brindled beast leaped at Torak's bare foot. Renn's bow sang. The dog fell with a gurgling yowl and an arrow through its throat.

Beside her, Dark let fly with his slingshot. A gray brute fell and did not stir again. Dark killed another with a stone that split its skull; Renn shot one in the chest. It staggered backward into the chasm, its yowls dying to nothing.

Two dogs streaked across the cavern, disappearing into a tunnel as if they'd scented prey. The remaining dog circled Torak's perch. A tokoroth appeared at its base and began to climb, a knife clamped between its teeth. Renn nocked her final arrow and took aim. Her hands shook. The creature was a demon, but it had the body of a child.

A stone whistled through the air. The tokoroth fell with a shriek, clutching a broken shin. Grimly, Dark reloaded his slingshot, but the tokoroth dragged itself into the shadows.

Peering into the haze, Renn sought another target. The smoke was too thick. Its fumes reached into her mind. She pictured the Masked One gloating over the fire-opal. *None can hinder Eostra.*

Renn set down her bow. So. This was not to be won with arrows.

Something of Saeunn's uncompromising will stiffened her resolve. You are a Mage, she told herself. Think like one.

Your spell is flawed, the Walker had said. *It holds the hair of a living man.*

Renn went still. She peered at the cord which netted

the fire-opal. It seemed to be braided with different-colored threads. She caught glints of black, russet, gold. . . .

Hair. Eostra had snared the spirits of the Soul-Eaters with their own hair. She had woven it into this cord which now bound the fire-opal, this cord which bound the dead Soul-Eaters to her—just as, with Torak's hair, she meant to bind his world-soul and take his power.

"Torak!" shouted Renn. *"Cut the cord!"*

Trapped in the Soul-Eater's marrow, Torak struggled to break free. His spirit was tiring. Eostra was too strong.

From a great distance, he heard someone shouting. It sounded like Renn. It couldn't be.

For an instant, the shouting distracted Eostra. Torak felt her will waver. It was enough. He seized his chance.

His eyes snapped open. He was back in his body. Someone was still shouting.

"Cut the cord that binds the fire-opal! Torak! Cut it and you'll break the spell! You'll send them away forever!"

It *was* Renn. He couldn't see her, but he saw one of her arrows, jutting from the throat of the brindled dog.

The cord. Strength coursed through him. He knew what to do.

Swiftly, he untied himself and slid down the pillar. A dog sprang from the murk. He thrust his knife in its belly and ripped. Kicking the carcass aside, he jabbed at the dark. No tokoroths, no dogs; though he heard the snarls of a savage fight. With his free hand he grabbed a stone and staggered toward the rock pile. Renn was right, there *was* a way. The spell could be broken, the Soul-Eaters banished forever. Why, then, was Eostra undeterred?

Once again, the fire was quenched and her chanting ceased. Through the drifting smoke, she spread her wings and summoned the last of the Unquiet Dead.

Wise as the wolf, the willful one . . .

No! Torak tried to shout, but his tongue stuck to the roof of his mouth. Helpless, he heard the Soul-Eater call the beloved name he hadn't spoken out loud for three summers.

For a moment there was silence.

The cave seemed to echo with the howls of unseen wolves. Behind the altar, smoke danced and drew together. A tall figure began to take shape.

Torak dropped his knife with a clatter. "Fa."

THIRTY-SEVEN

The figure in the smoke was as faint as moon-shadow on a cloudy night—but Torak knew. He knew as he stood gazing up at his father.

"Fa—it's me. Torak."

The dead white eyes stared down at him without recognition. His father's spirit belonged to Eostra.

Somewhere, Renn was shouting. "Cut the cord! Send them away forever!"

Send Fa away? Away forever?

He couldn't do it. He was twelve summers old: bewildered, terrified, watching his father bleed. Fa, don't die. *Please* don't die.

Tears slid down his cheeks as he stumbled toward the rock pile.

"Cut the cord!" shouted Renn.

"I can't," Torak whispered. "Fa . . . I can't lose you all over again."

He began to climb.

He heard the rattle of bones and the chant of the Soul-Eater. He felt a sudden sharp pain at the back of his scalp, and saw the owl fly off with a lock of his hair in its talons. It didn't matter. Nothing mattered except reaching Fa.

He stood in the bitter haze before the altar. Behind it the Masked One chanted, surrounded by the shadowy throng of the Unquiet Dead. He stretched out his hand toward his father. The figure in the smoke did not respond.

A vision flashed across Torak's mind of what might have been if Fa had lived: if they were still together, and the fire-opal had never existed. Grief twisted in his heart like a knife.

But the fire-opal *did* exist. There it was in the mace, throbbing like an open wound.

With a cry, Torak reached across the altar, seized the mace, and dragged it toward the flames.

The Soul-Eater's grip was stone. He couldn't do it.

With her other hand she raised her spear to strike. Torak lashed out with his rock. The spear clattered to the floor. A tokoroth fastened its jaws on his forearm. Renn's wrist-guard protected him. Again he brought down the rock, crushing the creature's skull like an eggshell. Still gripping the mace, he fought the Soul-Eater across the flames. He caught the glitter of her eyes behind the mask. He gave a desperate wrench and dashed the mace into the fire. Choking on the stink of burning hair, he raised the rock—and shattered the fire-opal to bloody shards.

With a shriek, Eostra plunged both hands into the flames, clawing out the fragments and holding them up. The last shreds of burning hair curled and shriveled to nothing.

The Unquiet Dead began to disintegrate. Through a mist of tears, Torak watched his father fade.

But in the final moment, the smoke face changed. It became Fa as he had been when he was alive, and it lit up as he saw his son. "*Torak* . . ." he murmured, as quiet as a sleeping breath.

Then he was gone.

Torak stood shaking before the altar. Some part of him knew that Eostra still held the fragments of the fire-opal. Some part of him heard her beginning to chant.

Eostra summons the spirit walker
Eostra binds him to her!

Far away, Renn was screaming a warning. "Torak!
Behind you!"

THIRTY-EIGHT

"Behind you!" screamed Renn. She was ready to shoot, but the tokoroth kept slipping into shadow, dragging its broken leg.

Torak appeared to come to himself at last. He saw the tokoroth crawling up the rock pile. He saw Eostra brandishing the fragments of the fire-opal and lifting her free hand to the eagle owl, which swooped toward her with the lock of his hair in its talons.

In the blink of an eye, the tokoroth sprang. Torak seized its arms and flung it bodily over his head. It came on again, relentless. They grappled, moving too fast—Renn couldn't get a clear shot. Beside her, Dark gripped his slingshot. Torak threw the tokoroth onto the altar. It twitched as its spine snapped—and slid off, dead.

Two black shapes came racing from the shadows, up the rock pile toward Torak. Renn and Dark let fly at the dogs. They hit the same target. The stricken creature scrabbled at the edge of the chasm, and fell with a howl. Torak turned and seemed to see the chasm for the first time. The other dog sprang.

Renn had no more arrows. Frantically, she searched for stones.

"None left," panted Dark. Grabbing her axe, he flung it with all his might. It struck short of the rock pile.

Torak was on his knees fighting the dog, his hands in its scruff, battling to keep its jaws from his face.

Renn beat the stones with her fists.

A silver arrow streaked across the cavern: Wolf racing to save his pack-brother. His sides were bloody, his white fangs gleamed, and his glare was more ferocious than Renn had ever seen. In a flying leap he was on them, sinking his teeth in the dog's throat, tearing it off Torak. Wolf and dog tumbled down the rocks, a snarling tangle of black and gray. Wolf sprang to his feet and stood panting, his pelt matted with blood. The dog lay still. Wolf had torn open its belly, spilling its guts.

The eagle owl swooped across the cavern, flying low to decoy him from Torak. Too low. As they disappeared into the dark, Renn saw Wolf snap at its wing and bring it down, savaging it to pieces.

Torak was leaning on the altar, utterly spent. Behind it, the Soul-Eater brandished the lock of his hair in triumph.

"Eostra binds him to her!" she shrieked. *"Eostra lives forever!"* Feeding the hair between her wooden lips, she snatched up her spear and thrust it at his chest.

He stumbled sideways. They circled the altar: Eostra jabbing, Torak staggering out of reach.

On the far side of the cavern, a shadow moved.

Renn caught her breath. In disbelief, she saw the Walker on all fours, shaking his head.

"Hidden Ones," he croaked.

Torak and the Soul-Eater went on circling the altar.

"Hidden People of the Mountain! The Walker calls on you! Rid the world of this canker!"

At first, Renn felt nothing.

Then: a faint tremor beneath her hands.

The Walker lifted his scrawny arms, his voice gathering strength. "The Walker calls on you! Let the jaws of the Mountain snap shut!"

In the cavern, the stone teeth shuddered. Renn saw a great, jutting pillar topple and fall with a crash.

"Rid us of the Soul-Eater forever!"

A hanging column thundered down upon the altar, splitting it in two. Still clutching the fragments of the fire-opal, Eostra staggered back from the ruins. She teetered on the brink of the chasm. With a terrible, unearthly cry, she lost her balance and fell.

But as she fell, her spear caught the hem of Torak's tunic.

In horror, Renn saw him pull back. The weight was too great. He had no knife to cut himself free.

"Torak!" Renn screamed.

Torak dropped to his knees.

The Soul-Eater dragged him with her into the chasm.

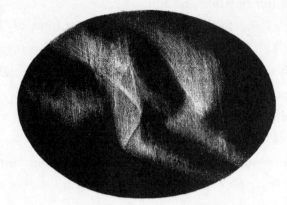

THIRTY-NINE

He is deep in the earth. It is cold and dark, and there is a roaring in his ears and a smell of rottenness in his nostrils. Is he already dead?

Someone is carrying him. They must be taking him to the bone-grounds.

Now they're laying him down, passing hands over his face, muttering a death chant. Leaving him alone.

The stars wheel above him. Moons rise and set and rise again. All that has been, and is, and will be flows through him. He is a baby in the Den, suckling his wolf mother. He is running from the clearing where Fa lies dying. He is falling into the chasm in the Mountain of Ghosts.

He is back beneath the stars. Small, shadowy people are bending over him. He gazes up into strange, gray, pointed faces and moon-bright eyes.

Where's Renn? he tries to ask. Where's Wolf?

The eyes blink out. Once again, he is alone.

Still the stars wheel above him. *Coldest of all, the darkest light.* The last light a man sees before he dies.

He feels no pain; only a great emptiness. He doesn't want to die alone.

But he is so tired.

He stands looking down at his body. He doesn't want to leave, but he has to, he is so tired. With a reluctant sigh, he turns and begins to climb toward the stars.

The First Tree was shining brighter than Renn had ever seen. The whole sky was alive with rippling, shimmering green, waiting to welcome Torak's spirit.

The white-haired boy drew the hanging across the mouth of his cave and made her sit by the fire, where he wrapped a woolly mantle around her shoulders and put a steaming beaker in her hands. She was shaking so hard that she spilled most of it. Torak and Wolf were gone. They had left her behind in the emptiness.

Numbly, she took in the white stone creatures peering

254 CHRONICLES OF ANCIENT DARKNESS

from every crack. Nothing was real. Not this cave, not that nightmare rush through the tunnel, with the rocks falling and Dark dragging her to safety. Torak was dead. Not real.

On the other side of the fire, the ravens—the white and the black—awoke, and irritably snapped their wings.

"It was the ghosts that woke them," said Dark, warming his hands at the fire. "Most have gone to be with their clans, but a few always get left behind." He went on talking—something about his sister not being here, so maybe this time she'd found peace in the sky— but Renn had stopped listening.

Souls' Night. She pictured the Mountain clans feasting with their dead; and her own clan, far away in the Forest. Perhaps already they'd sensed that the menace of Eostra was ended.

"Renn," said Dark, wrenching her back. "He'd put on the Death Marks. At least his souls will stay together."

But he hasn't got a guardian, she thought bleakly. So who will come for him and guide him up to the First Tree?

Wolf watched the last of the Walking Breaths disappear down the gorge.

He'd followed them out of the Mountain, hoping they would lead him to Tall Tailless. They hadn't. Now he stood in the howling Dark, with the wind clawing his fur and snatching the scents away.

Wolf was frightened. This was different from the other times when he and his pack-brother had been parted. This was as if a great Fast Wet was rushing between them: one that couldn't be crossed.

Whimpering, Wolf raced over the Bright Soft Cold and back again.

Above the yowling of wind and Wet, he caught a whine so high that it was like hearing light. He knew that whine. It was the voice of the deer bone which Tall Tailless carried at his flank: the deer bone which held the dusty earth that he sometimes smeared on Wolf. The deer bone which, once before, in the Forest, Wolf had heard sing.

Eagerly, Wolf sped after the singing: down the slope, past where they had fought the dogs, toward the Fast Wet which bubbled from the Mountain.

Tall Tailless lay beside it.

Wolf pounced on his chest and licked his nose. *Wake up!* Tall Tailless didn't move.

Wolf barked in his ears. He scrabbled and pawed, he nipped the cold face. No response.

Wolf's world broke apart. *No. No. Tall Tailless was Not-Breath!*

But the horn was still singing.

The singing sank deep into Wolf and became the strange, clear certainty which came to him at times. At last he knew what to do.

Filled with new purpose, he cast about for the scent. There: faint, but very familiar. The scent of his pack-brother. Wolf loped after it.

He hadn't gone far up the Mountain when he saw it. It was the same size and shape as Tall Tailless, but a bit fuzzy at the edges: the Breath-that-Walks.

Wolf sensed that it was lost and confused. He slowed to a trot, so as not to startle it, and wagged his tail. It saw him and stood, swaying and blinking. Wolf leaned against its legs and gave it a gentle push. The Breath-that-Walks staggered. Nudging it along, Wolf guided it down the slope. When at last they reached the body, he nosed it back inside.

Tall Tailless gave a shuddering gasp—and breathed.

Wolf licked his pack-brother's face to warm him up, then lay down on top of him, to make quite sure that this time, the Breath-that-Walks stayed in.

Dark said he was going to fetch Renn's gear that she'd left on the Mountain, and maybe she should come too, as seeing the sun come up might make her feel a bit better—it sometimes helped him.

It had snowed in the night. Eostra's dead cold was gone. The ravens chased one other through the shining sky, and the new snow sparkled gold in the rising sun.

Dark was wrong. This didn't help. It was her first dawn without Torak.

As she crunched along in Dark's trail, she thought of the long journey before her, back to the Forest. She would have to tell everyone what had happened. And with Saeunn dead, they would want her to be the Raven Mage. A life of aching loneliness stretched ahead. She couldn't bear it.

They neared Torak's old snow hole, and Dark went in search of her gear.

"Something odd," he said when he came back.

Renn couldn't bring herself to care, but he was shyly insistent, so she let him show her what he'd found.

Big, blunt footprints in the snow.

She thought, so the Walker found a way out. That's good. But she couldn't feel it.

The white raven gave a deafening croak, and veered west.

Dark hurried off in pursuit. Renn stayed where she was.

The raven's wings flashed like ice as she flew down to a stream bubbling from a small cave in the boulder field. Settling on a snow-covered hillock, the raven fluffed up her chin-feathers and cawed, exhaling little puffs of frosty breath.

"Renn," called Dark.

Renn kneaded her temples. What now?

The white raven lifted off sharply as the hillock heaved, and Wolf burst out, shook the snow off his pelt, and bounded toward her.

"*Wolf.*" Her voice cracked. She floundered down the slope. Wolf leaped at her, knocking her backward and covering her in slobbery wolf kisses. She flung her arms around him, but he squirmed away and loped back to Dark.

The white raven was still cawing, and now Rip and Rek were joining in. Wolf was lashing his tail as he bounded in circles around the hillock, and Dark was sinking to his knees beside it, shouting, "Renn! It's Torak! He's *alive*!"

FORTY

The cub woke with a start. Those were wolf howls!

No they weren't. It was only the ravens making wolf noises. They did that a lot. They laughed when the cub raced about, searching for his pack.

Crossly, he slumped down and flipped his tail over his nose. But he couldn't get back to sleep. He was too hungry.

Crawling out from under the rock, he stood at the mouth of the Den and snuffed the air.

The Light had come, but not the ravens; so no chance of any meat. It was warmer, and the Bright Soft Cold was deeper. From where the cub stood, the white hill dropped steeply, then rose again to make the Mountain. Even that looked kinder. Once, the cub had tried to reach it, but the ravens had driven him back. He'd been annoyed. Then he'd heard the baying on the Mountain: dreadful, angry dogs who sounded as if they ate wolf cubs. He hadn't tried again.

Blinking in the glare, the cub padded out into the Bright Soft Cold—and sank to his belly. Anxiously, he scanned the Up for the terrible owl. Nothing. Maybe the big tailless had scared it away.

The big tailless had come in the Dark, when the cub—who'd been trying to hunt lemmings—had fallen into a hole and couldn't get out. The cub had been yowling for a long time when the big tailless had peered in. He had a rich, reassuring smell, so the cub had wagged his tail. The big tailless had scooped him out, tossed him a scrap of beautiful slimy meat, and shambled off.

It was very quiet on the hill. Even the wind was gone. The stillness was frightening.

The cub barked. *I'm here!*

Nothing replied. The cub began to whimper. He missed his pack so much that it hurt.

Suddenly, he stopped whimpering. In the distance he heard the deep, echoing croaks of ravens. He swiveled his ears. Those were *his* ravens!

He yowled.

They didn't come.

Well, then, he would go to them.

Eagerly, he bounded through the Bright Soft Cold. It broke beneath him and he tumbled down the hill.

At the bottom, he righted himself and sneezed. The Den was high above, unclimbably high. Now what to do?

Somewhere in the hills, a wolf howled.

The cub sprang alert. This wasn't a raven trick, this really was a wolf. *It was his mother!*

Frantically, the cub barked. *I'm here! I'm here!*

The howling stopped.

The cub barked and barked as he floundered through the Bright Soft Cold. *I'm here!*

He was beginning to tire when a dark shadow came rushing down the hill—and suddenly his mother was pouncing on him and they were rolling together and she was whining and nuzzling and he was mewing and burying himself in her wonderful warm fur, snuffling up her beloved, strong, meaty mother smell. Then she sicked up some food and he gulped it down, while she gave him a thorough licking all over. After that they leaned against each other and howled their happiness to the Up.

The cub was still howling when his mother gave a whine and shot away.

The cub stopped in midhowl and opened his eyes.

And there was his father, racing toward them over the Bright Soft Cold.

FORTY-ONE

It's summer, and Renn walks with Torak under the murmuring trees.

"Don't go," she says.

Torak turns to her and smiles, and she sees the little green flecks in his eyes. "But Renn," he says. "The Forest goes on forever. I saw it from the Mountain."

"Please. I can't bear it."

He touches her cheek and walks away.

Renn bit her knuckle and curled deeper in her sleeping-sack.

It might never happen, she told herself. Everything is fine.

Lying on her side, she watched the firelight rippling over the cross-beams. She was back in the Forest, in the big shelter where the Raven Clan lived together in midwinter. All was familiar: the tree-trunk walls plugged with moss, the reindeer-hide roof open to the stars above the fire. She smelled woodsmoke. She heard the crackle of flames and the low hum of voices.

You are safe with your clan, she told herself. The Dark Time is over, the sun has come back. The Red Deer are camped nearby, and Torak is . . .

She sat up. In the gloom, she couldn't see him.

But that wasn't unusual. With the days still very short, most hunting was done at night, by the light of the moon and the First Tree.

Around her, people sat calmly sewing or knapping flint. Three moons had passed since Souls' Night. To the clans of the Open Forest, Eostra and the shadow sickness were only a memory.

Pulling on her clothes, Renn went to find Dark.

His white hair glowed at the other end of the shelter, where he sat on the edge of the sleeping platform, intent on a carving. Durrain, the Red Deer Mage, was talking to him as she marked out a jerkin on a reindeer-hide with a piece of charcoal.

Renn asked if they'd seen Torak. Dark said he thought he'd gone to find the wolves. Abruptly, Renn turned her back on him and pretended to warm her hands at the fire.

"What's wrong?" said Durrain.

"Nothing," lied Renn.

She wouldn't have thought it possible that she could miss the Mountains, but she did. She missed those first days in Dark's cave; and later, with the Swans and the Mountain Hare Clan. Torak had healed slowly in body and spirit, but she had been with him. He'd told her how Wolf had brought him back from the dead, and about his father. She'd told him about the Walker, and Saeunn's last gift to her in the Mountain. They had discussed Eostra's Magecraft, and decided that it was the earthblood from his mother's medicine horn which had protected his world-soul. They had been together when he'd left his father's seal amulet as an offering for the Hidden People; and when she'd helped the Mountain Mages chase the demons back to the Otherworld—and then stayed to perform a rite for the souls of the tokoroth children; because if things had been different, she too would have been a tokoroth.

Through it all, they had been side by side. But since they'd got back to the Forest, that had changed.

"Renn?" said Dark.

"What?" she snapped.

"Shall we go and look for him?"

"Oh, leave me *alone*!"

Ignoring Dark's hurt smile and Durrain's reproachful glance, she stomped off to fetch her bow.

"Ah, Renn." Fin-Kedinn sat on the other side of the fire, making arrows. "Help me with these, will you?"

"I'm going hunting."

"Do this first."

Blowing out a long breath, she threw down her bow.

Her uncle had already smoothed the alderwood shafts and secured the flint heads with sinew. Piles of halved wood-grouse feathers lay beside him, sorted into left and right wing, and he was binding them in threes to the shafts. A large dog leaned companionably against his calf.

Fin-Kedinn asked why Renn was angry, and she said she wasn't.

Why, she thought, does he want me to say it? He knows what's wrong. Torak never seems to be around. And people keep bowing to me as if I was already the new Raven Mage—which I'm *not*, not till I say yes.

As if he'd guessed her thoughts, Fin-Kedinn said, "You've been back some time, yet you've never asked how the ancient one died."

Ignoring him, Renn trimmed an arrow with her knife, leaving just enough feather to make it fly straight.

"It was just after I'd returned from the fells," began the Raven Leader. "She'd waited till she knew I was back to keep the clans together. She chose a still, cold day; a grove of hollies half a daywalk from camp. We laid her in the snow in her sleeping-sack, and she drank the potion she'd prepared to make her drowsy. We sang to the ancestors to tell them she was coming, then she told us to leave. She made a good death."

Renn set down her knife. "I know why you're telling me this. The same reason you got Durrain to stay. To make sure I take her place."

Fin-Kedinn regarded her steadily. "Is that why you're scared?"

"I'm not scared!" she flung back.

The dog flattened his ears and pressed against Fin-Kedinn.

Renn glowered at the fire. "It's not fair!" she blurted out. "They bow to me and call me Mage, but they're frightened of him. Some even make the sign of the hand to ward him off."

"He came back from the dead, Renn. Of course they're uneasy. But they do know what they owe him."

"Oh, yes," she said drily. "They've even started telling stories about him: the Listener who talks with wolves and ravens. They just don't want him living with them."

"And Torak. What does he want?"

As always, he'd sensed what really troubled her. "I don't know," she said miserably.

Fin-Kedinn ran his thumb along an arrowshaft.

"They say that in the Beginning, all people were like Torak, and knew the souls of other creatures. Now it's only him. Durrain thinks he may be the last. That in times to come, there will be no more spirit walkers; and all that remains will be the friendship between man and dog: a memory of what once was." He paused. "Torak is one apart, Renn. The clans know it. He knows it."

Renn sprang to her feet. "Even *you*? You want him gone?"

"*Want?*" Fin-Kedinn's blue eyes blazed. "You think I *want* him to leave?"

"Then tell him to stay!"

"No," said the Raven Leader. "He has to find his own way."

Fin-Kedinn caught Torak as he was heading off to find Wolf, and told him to come with him up-valley to check the snares. Torak was about to protest, but something in his foster father's voice made him think better of it.

Dawn was still far off, but the moon was bright, and the trees threw long blue shadows across the frozen river. Torak and Fin-Kedinn crunched over the ice in a haze of frosty breath. On the opposite bank, a reindeer stopped pawing the snow to watch them pass, then went back to munching lichen.

Belatedly, Torak noticed that Fin-Kedinn carried a food pouch and bedding roll; he asked if he should have brought his too. Fin-Kedinn said no. Some time later, he turned up a side gully.

"But the snares are upriver," said Torak.

Fin-Kedinn continued to climb.

The snow was deeper in the gully. Trees which had been snapped in the ice storm cast weird, humped shadows in the moonlight.

The Walker sat beneath a broken holly, retying his foot-bindings.

Torak halted. It seemed impossible that this ragged ruin of a man had once been a great Mage. Only Fin-Kedinn had seen deep into the Walker's heart, and perceived that he still possessed the skill and the spark of sanity which would drive him to cross the fells and find Eostra's lair. The Raven Leader's faith had not been misplaced.

Fin-Kedinn put his fists to his chest in sign of friendship. "Narrander," he said quietly.

The Walker ignored him.

Cautiously, Torak went to squat beside him. "Walker," he said. "You saved my life. Thank you."

"What? What?" snapped the old man.

"You carried me out of the Mountain. You covered my hands and feet so I wouldn't get frostbite."

The Walker clawed a louse from his beard, squashed it between finger and thumb, and ate it. "Hidden Ones saved the wolf boy. The Walker just pulled him out."

Munching another louse, he gave a spluttery laugh. "A rock cut the Masked One in two, like a wasp! Now where's Narik?"

Fin-Kedinn approached. "Come with us to camp, Narrander. You'll be warm. We'll look after you."

The Walker drew his moldering hides around him and waved the Raven Leader away. "Narik and the Walker are off to their beautiful valley. They look after themselves."

Fin-Kedinn sighed, and set down his bundles. "Clothes. Food. They're yours, old friend."

"Clothes, food," mimicked the Walker. "But where's Narik?"

Fin-Kedinn hesitated. "Narik died in the great fire," he said gently. "You remember. Your son died."

Torak stared at him.

"Ah, *here* is Narik!" cried the Walker, pulling a sleepy-looking snow-vole from his cape.

Torak said slowly, "Walker. You told me once that you lost your eye in an accident, knapping flint. But did you lose it in the great fire, when my father shattered the fire-opal?"

The old man stroked the vole with a grimy finger. "It popped right out," he crooned, "and a raven ate it. Ravens like eyes."

Fin-Kedinn regarded him gravely. "You've avenged Narik's death. You helped end the terror of the Eagle

Owl Mage. Come with us. Be at peace."

The old man went on crooning as if he hadn't heard.

Fin-Kedinn indicated to Torak that they should leave. To the Walker he said, "Farewell, Narrander. May the guardian swim with you."

As they rose to go, the Walker flashed out a claw and dragged Torak back. His grip was strong. Torak caught a blast of foul breath, and saw something flicker in the single eye, like a minnow in a murky pond. "The wolf boy's troubled, eh? Bits of souls sticking to his spirit? The Great Wanderer, the Forest, the Masked One? He's like the Walker, yes, he got too close, so he has to keep moving!"

With a cry, Torak pulled free. The Walker gave a bubbling laugh which ended in a cough.

They left him in the moonlight among the broken trees, clutching the snow-vole to his breast.

Neither of them spoke on their way to the snares. When they got there, they found three willow grouse and two hares stiffening in the snow. Fin-Kedinn plucked one of the grouse, while Torak woke a fire and set a flat stone to heat. Fin-Kedinn split the grouse and laid it on the stone. When they'd eaten, he took an antler point from his belt and started sharpening his knife.

After a while, he said, "I told you once that the seventh Soul-Eater had died in the fire. I told you that because I'd sworn to Narrander not to reveal that he'd survived."

Torak took this in silence. Then he said, "Narik. His *son?*"

Fin-Kedinn paused. Then he told the story which Torak's father had told him the night after it happened.

"Narik was eight summers old when Narrander joined the Healers. Narrander soon wanted to leave. They wouldn't let him. He was stubborn. To make him obey, the Eagle Owl Mage took Narik." He shook his head. "Souls' Night. Your father summoned them to what would become the Burnt Hill. He woke the great fire. Shattered the fire-opal. The Seal Mage was terribly burned. The Walker lost an eye. All escaped with their lives . . . except Narik. Bound, hidden by the Masked One. His father found the body. He went mad with grief."

Embers spat. A gray owl swept past on its way to hunt.

Raising his head, Torak watched the lights of the First Tree fade as dawn approached. He thought of Narik and Narrander, and his father and mother; and of the brilliant, flawed Mages who had become the Soul-Eaters. So much suffering. And for what?

"It's over, Torak," Fin-Kedinn said softly.

"I know. But I thought—I thought I'd feel better."

"It takes time."

"How long?"

The Raven Leader spread his hands. "After your mother died, it took many winters for my spirit to heal."

"What brought you back?"

"Caring for my clan. Looking after Renn."

Her name hung between them in the frosty air.

Torak got up and walked away, then returned. "I know she has to stay. And maybe the Walker's right, maybe I will always be a wanderer. But I can't . . . I don't want to lose her."

He needed Fin-Kedinn to make things better; but the Raven Leader's face was hard as he sheathed his knife. "I'll take the prey back to camp," he said brusquely. "You put the fire to sleep and see to the fishing lines on the river."

Renn had forgotten to take any food with her, so by dawn she was hungry and bad-tempered. She hadn't found Torak, though she'd seen plenty of wolf tracks; and she felt awful about Dark.

The Mountain clans had only tolerated him because he was with Torak, and they'd made him sleep in a separate shelter at the edge of their camp. The Raven Clan, too, had been wary at first, though they'd changed when they'd seen Ark; a boy with a white raven deserved respect. Dark himself had taken instantly to the Forest, and adored being among people. But yesterday, Renn had found him anxiously fingering the small slate musk ox he'd brought from his cave. She'd reminded him that Fin-Kedinn had said he could stay as long as he liked, and he'd nodded politely; but she could see that he didn't really believe it, and dreaded being told to leave.

And you were nasty to him, she berated herself as she plodded toward camp. *Very clever, Renn. Just what he needs.*

Torak was on the river, hacking open ice holes with an antler pick and drawing in the lines. A pile of whitefish lay beside him, rapidly freezing, and Rip and Rek were walking about, pretending they weren't interested.

Torak glanced at Renn as she approached, then resumed his work.

Unlike her, he still wore his Mountain Hare tunic, drawn in at the waist by the belt Krukoslik had given him as a parting gift: a broad band of buckskin, sewn with many rows of reindeer teeth. Renn thought he looked good, not like anyone in the Open Forest. She asked him if he didn't mind appearing so different from everyone else.

"Why should I?" he said with a shrug. "It's what I am."

She picked up the antler and scratched the ice. "Don't you even care?"

"What's the point? I can't change it."

For a moment, he truly seemed a stranger to her: a tall young man in outlandish furs, with an outcast tattoo on his forehead and unsettling light-gray eyes. She thought, *Fin-Kedinn's right, he is apart. He always will be.*

Out loud, she said, "I need you to promise something."

He threw her a wary look. "What?"

She'd intended to ask him not to leave the clan, but instead she blurted out, "Don't ever spirit walk in me."

"*What?*" He flushed the color of beechnuts. "But—I'd never . . . I mean, why would I? I already know what you think."

Renn stared at him. "You—*know* what I think?"

He swallowed. ". . . Yes. In a way."

She flung down the antler and stalked off.

"Renn . . ."

The snowball hit him full in the face.

"There!" she shouted. "You didn't know I'd do that, did you?"

Torak was blinking and spitting out snow. His expression turned thoughtful. Renn decided she'd better run.

As she sped up the bank, she heard him coming after her. She ducked. His snowball missed her and hit Dark, who'd come to investigate the shouting.

Dark was astonished. "Wh-at . . ."

"It's a game!" panted Renn as she raced past, yelping as Torak's next missile struck her hard on the shoulder.

Dark caught on fast, and soon the air was thick with snowballs. Renn's aim was good, Dark's was better. Torak's was the worst, but he made up for it by relentless firing.

The ravens' excited caws brought the wolves bounding out of the Forest. Wolf made great twisting leaps and snapped snowballs in midair; Darkfur got spattered all over, as she was such an easy target; and Pebble raced about, barking and getting under everyone's feet. Eventually, Torak and Renn ganged up on Dark and pelted him until he laughed so much he fell over. Gasping and clutching their sides, Torak and Renn collapsed beside him, Wolf and Darkfur crashed into them, and Pebble climbed on top.

They lay gazing up at the sky, munching some hazel cakes Dark had brought with him, and tossing crumbs to the ravens. Then a cloud drifted over the sun, and it was suddenly cold.

Pebble wandered off and got entangled in a fishing line. Dark went to help him, followed by Wolf and his mate.

Renn flipped onto her belly and looked at Torak. "If you're going to leave," she said quickly, "get it over with."

Torak sat up. "Renn . . ."

"Well?"

He frowned. "Renn."

She got to her feet and walked away.

The wolves went to hunt in the Forest, and the others returned to camp: bedraggled, covered in snow, and having forgotten the whitefish on the ice.

Fin-Kedinn glanced from Torak to Renn, then told Torak to go and fetch the fish, and Renn to find Durrain, who was asking for her. "Dark, stay with me," he said curtly. "I need to talk to you."

Oh, no, thought Renn. She saw Torak hanging back, worried for his friend.

"I'll fetch my gear," said Dark in a defeated voice.

"Why?" Fin-Kedinn said sharply. "Are you leaving?"

"Um. But I thought . . ."

"Do you want to leave?"

Dark shook his head.

"Then stay."

"D-do you mean for good?"

"You belong with us. Yes?"

Shyly, Dark nodded.

"Well, then stay." Without waiting for a response, Fin-Kedinn turned on his heel and walked off.

Stunned, Dark watched him go. Torak grinned and clapped him on the shoulder. Renn wondered why her uncle wasn't smiling.

That night, she woke to see him sitting hunched by the fire. Unusually for Fin-Kedinn, he wasn't doing anything; he was simply staring into the flames.

In the Forest, the wolves howled. Renn made out Wolf's strong, happy song, and Darkfur's musical howls, and Pebble's ever-improving yowl.

She watched Fin-Kedinn turn his head to listen. His

expression was sad: as if the wolves were telling him something he didn't want to hear.

After a while, he sat straighter, and squared his shoulders.

And nodded once.

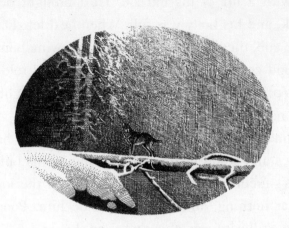

FORTY-TWO

The Dark was gathering under the trees as Wolf trotted through the Bright Soft Cold to wait for his pack-brother.

He reached the hill above the great Den of the taillesses, and jumped onto a log to catch the smells. He watched some of the raven-smelling pack emerge from the Forest with piles of branches in their forepaws. The white raven lit onto the top of the Den, and the kind tailless with the pale head-fur came out and called it down.

The black ravens flew past Wolf and greeted him with soft *gro-gro*s. As he was in a good mood, he acknowledged them with a lift of his muzzle. He'd brought down a roebuck, and his belly was full. When he'd left Darkfur and the cub, they'd been comfortably gnawing bones.

A loud crunching in the Bright Soft Cold told Wolf that his pack-brother was coming. So noisy, thought Wolf affectionately.

To make sure that Tall Tailless saw him, he left the trees and stood in the open, swinging his tail. Tall Tailless's greeting was subdued. He sat on the log and stared at nothing, and Wolf sat beside him. Poor Tall Tailless. Still confused about what he should do.

They were silent for a while. Then Tall Tailless said, *Your Breath-that-Walks. I saw it on the Mountain. It shines very bright.*

At least, that was what Wolf thought he said. Sometimes it was hard to tell.

You are wise, Tall Tailless went on. *You always help. Help me now. Should I stay with the raven pack? Or leave?*

Wolf put his head on his pack-brother's knee, and met his gaze. And told him.

Next morning, Torak was tying his sleeping-sack roll when Dark appeared at the door of the shelter. They exchanged glances, and Torak saw with relief that he didn't have to explain to his friend.

"I'll miss you," said Dark.

Torak tried to smile. "My father used to say that the best thing in life is moving on to the next campsite." He paused. "Of course, that's a Wolf Clan saying, and I'm not Wolf Clan."

"Well. I'm not Raven Clan. They don't seem to mind."

"Do you know that some people are already calling you the White Raven?"

Dark smiled. Recently, he had gained a new assurance. Torak thought it suited him.

"What will you do?" said Dark.

"Oh . . . hunt. See parts of the Forest I've never seen before. Be with Wolf and Darkfur and Pebble." He thought for a moment. "I'm tired, Dark. I want to be at peace among trees."

Dark nodded. "Renn says that too much has happened to you; and not enough to me."

Torak looked down at his sleeping-sack and thought, trust Renn to understand. Scowling, he yanked the last knot tight.

"Here," said Dark, holding out his palm. "You haven't got an amulet, so I made you one."

It was a small stone wolf on a thong: beautifully carved in gray slate, its eyes half-closed as it lifted its tiny muzzle to howl. "I've scratched the Forest mark on his belly," said Dark, "and I reddened it with alder blood. That's quite important. The red is for fire and the Mountains, and friendship. You should renew it from time to time. The alder blood, I mean."

Torak took the amulet and put it around his neck. "Thanks," he said. "I will."

He found Fin-Kedinn sitting by the river, mending fishing nets. The Raven Leader stopped working and watched him approach. "I wish you didn't have to leave," he said quietly.

"So do I. But my pack-brother reminded me of something. That a wolf cannot be of two packs."

Fin-Kedinn nodded thoughtfully. "You know, when you were small, and your father sought out the ancient one at the clan meet by the Sea, he said to her, *Although my son isn't Wolf Clan, I think he is truly wolf.* I finally understand what he meant."

Torak's throat worked. "Fin-Kedinn. I don't—I don't know how to thank you for all you've done."

The Raven Leader frowned. "Don't thank me. Just remember, Torak. Wherever you go, you'll find friends among the clans. And I hope . . . I hope someday you'll come back."

"I will. I will see you again. I promise. My foster father."

Fin-Kedinn rose to his feet. His blue eyes glittered as he put his hand on the back of Torak's neck. They touched foreheads. "Good-bye, my son," said the Raven

Leader. "May your guardian run with you."

Torak left him and walked blindly out of camp.

It was a calm, sunny day in the Willow Grouse Moon, and although spring had not yet come, the Forest was beginning to stir. A woodpecker drummed in the distance. A tough little bullfinch perched in an ash tree, cracking seeds in its bill. A white hare sat on its hind legs to nibble frost-blackened haws.

Torak hadn't gone far when Wolf appeared and trotted beside him. His fur was spangled with snow, and his amber eyes were bright. Torak asked him where the pack-sister was, and Wolf led him halfway up the side of the valley.

Renn sat on a rock in a patch of sun, restringing her bow. Darkfur lay beside her, running her jaws over a bramble branch to clean them, while Rip and Rek perched in a tree, throwing pinecones at Pebble.

Darkfur and the cub came bounding over to greet them. Renn didn't even turn her head. Her hood was thrown back, and her red hair flamed. Torak paused to fix the image in his memory.

"I came to say good-bye," he said at last.

She glanced at him, then went back to her bow. "To whom?"

"Renn. I can't stay. And you can't leave."

"And if I could, you'd want to spare me the choice."

He did not reply.

Renn stood up and faced him, very pale and composed. "It's not your choice to make. It's mine."

Something in the way she said it made his heart skip a beat. "But . . . you're going to be the Clan Mage."

"No. That will be Dark."

Dark.

"Fin-Kedinn saw it before anyone," said Renn with a break in her voice. "That's why he got Durrain to stay. Not for me, but for Dark. She says he has amazing skill. And he wants it, he really does." Two spots of color had appeared on her cheeks. "Fin-Kedinn saw it all. He . . ." She swallowed. "He gave me the choice."

It was then that Torak saw the rest of her gear piled behind the rock.

"Torak," Renn said sternly. "You've tried to leave me behind before. This is *the last time.* Do you want me to come with you or not?"

Torak tried to speak, but he couldn't. He nodded.

"Say it," commanded Renn.

". . . Yes. Yes I want you to come with me."

She began to smile.

"Yes!" he shouted, lifting her in his arms and swinging her around so that her red hair flew, while the ravens burst into the air in a flurry of wings, and the wolves lashed their tails and howled.

Down in the valley, Fin-Kedinn heard them, rose to his feet, and raised his staff in farewell.

Torak and Renn jumped onto the rock so that Fin-Kedinn could see them, and waved their bows above their heads.

Then they grabbed Renn's gear and headed off into the morning, with the wolves trotting behind them, and the ravens sky-dancing overhead.

The CHRONICLES OF ANCIENT DARKNESS tell of Torak's adventures in the Forest and beyond, and of his quest to vanquish the Soul-Eaters. *Wolf Brother* is the first book, *Spirit Walker* the second, *Soul Eater* the third, *Outcast* the fourth, and *Oath Breaker* the fifth. *Ghost Hunter* is the sixth and final book.

AUTHOR'S NOTE

Torak's world is the world of six thousand years ago: after the Ice Age, but before the spread of farming to his part of northwest Europe, when the land was one vast Forest.

The people of Torak's world looked pretty much like you or me, but their way of life was very different. They didn't have writing, metals, or the wheel, but they didn't need them. They were superb survivors. They knew all about the animals, trees, plants, and rocks around them. When they wanted something, they knew where to find it, or how to make it.

They lived in small clans, and many of them moved a lot: some staying in camp for just a few days, like the Wolf Clan; others staying for a whole moon or a season, like the Raven and Boar Clans; while others stayed put all year round, like the Seal Clan. Thus some of the clans have moved since the events in *Oath Breaker*, as you'll see from the slightly amended map.

When I was researching *Ghost Hunter*, I visited Finnish Lapland in midwinter. There, in the Urkho Kekkonen National Park (part of the Saariselkä Wilderness), I snowshoed for miles, following the trail of an elk, and watched reindeer happily pawing the snow off lichen in temperatures of zero degrees Fahrenheit.

I also spent time in the Dovrefjell highlands in Norway, where, on many solo hikes, I got the feel of the fells, and experienced that strange, haunting feeling of being alone in the mountains. On many occasions I observed musk oxen, which resemble extremely shaggy bison, but are in fact related to sheep. I gathered scraps of their incredibly warm wool, which they'd left behind snagged on branches; and I often had to alter the course of my hikes when a herd of musk oxen blocked my path. I also climbed the slopes of Mount Snøhetta (7,500 feet). Its sudden fogs, eerie crags, and treacherous boulder field gave me much inspiration for the Mountain of Ghosts.

Finally, I have, of course, kept up my friendship with the wolves of the UK Wolf Conservation Trust, who continue to inspire me. It's been a privilege to spend time with wolves whom I first knew as cubs, and who are now happy, healthy, boisterous young adults, thanks to their devoted carers.

I'd like to thank everyone at the UK Wolf Conservation Trust for letting me befriend the wolves; Mr. Derrick

Coyle, the (now retired) Yeoman Ravenmaster of the Tower of London, whose extensive knowledge and experience of the ravens there has been a continual inspiration; the friendly and helpful people of the district of Ivalo in Finland; Ellen and Knut Nyhus of the Kongsvold Fjeldstue, Dovrefjell, particularly for getting me across the army firing range to the foot of Snøhetta, thus enabling me to climb it (almost) to the top.

I want to thank everyone at my publishers, the Orion Publishing Group, for their wholehearted support of these books right from the start. I'm also extremely grateful to Geoff Taylor for creating the gorgeous chapter illustrations and evocative endpaper maps.

As always, my thanks go to my agent, Peter Cox, for encouraging the idea from the very beginning, and for supporting it so tirelessly and skillfully throughout.

Lastly, my special thanks to Fiona Kennedy, who has encouraged me in the writing of these books with such boundless imagination, talent, patience, commitment, and understanding. I could not ask for a better publisher and editor.

MICHELLE PAVER
2009

Find out more about the

CHRONICLES OF ANCIENT DARKNESS

at www.chroniclesofancientdarkness.com.

Explore Torak's world, read excerpts from the book,
and take the Clan Quiz.

Visit Michelle Paver's website at
www.michellepaver.com and meet other
readers of *Ghost Hunter* at the official
worldwide fan site, www.torak.info.

MICHELLE PAVER

was born in central Africa but went to England as a child. After earning a degree in biochemistry from Oxford University, she became a partner in a London law firm but eventually gave that up to write full-time.

The Chronicles of Ancient Darkness series came from Michelle's lifelong passion for animals, anthropology, and the distant past—as well as an encounter with a large bear in a remote valley in Southern California. To research the books, Michelle has traveled to Finland, Greenland, Sweden, Norway, Arctic Canada, Poland, and the Carpathian Mountains. She has slept on reindeer skins, swum with wild killer whales, and gotten nose to nose with polar bears—and, of course, wolves. The books have been made into widely acclaimed audiobooks, read by Ian McKellen.